Where am I?

I back away, step onto grass. It's cold and wet against my feet, sends a chill crawling through my toes and up my spine.

Walking, I am walking, almost running, off the grass and onto a road, the streetlight beaming at the end of it, glowing over a sign. Homeway Lane.

Where am I?

Street, alley, driveway, walk, road, I know.

I don't know Homeway Lane.

Where am I?

Close my eyes, this is just a dream, a weird, bad dream, like—

I don't know.

I don't know any of my bad dreams. I don't know—

I open my eyes.

It's still dark, still night, my skin is cold and I have goose bumps, but this isn't real, it's just a dream, a bad dream and I know that just like I know that I am—I am—I am—

I don't know.

I don't know.

→ OTHER BOOKS YOU MAY ENJOY ←

WITHDRAWN

as i wake

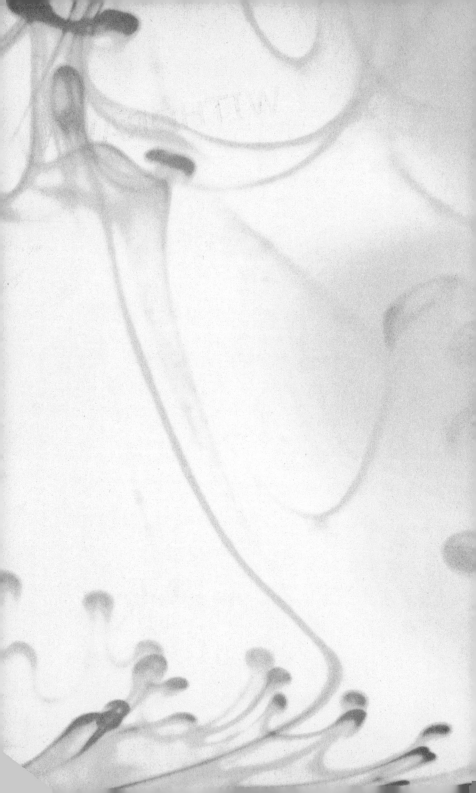

ELIZABETH SCOTT

as i wake

speak

An Imprint of Penguin Group (USA) Inc.

SPEAK

Published by the Penguin Group

Penguin Group (USA) Inc., 345 Hudson Street, New York, New York 10014, U.S.A.

Penguin Group (Canada), 90 Eglinton Avenue East, Suite 700, Toronto, Ontario, Canada M4P 2Y3

(a division of Pearson Penguin Canada Inc.)

Penguin Books Ltd, 80 Strand, London WC2R 0RL, England

Penguin Ireland, 25 St Stephen's Green, Dublin 2, Ireland (a division of Penguin Books Ltd)

Penguin Group (Australia), 250 Camberwell Road, Camberwell, Victoria 3124, Australia

(a division of Pearson Australia Group Pty Ltd)

Penguin Books India Pvt Ltd, 11 Community Centre,

Panchsheel Park, New Delhi - 110 017, India

Penguin Group (NZ), 67 Apollo Drive, Rosedale, Auckland, New Zealand

(a division of Pearson New Zealand Ltd.)

Penguin Books (South Africa) (Pty) Ltd, 24 Sturdee Avenue,

Rosebank, Johannesburg 2196, South Africa

Penguin Books Ltd, Registered Offices: 80 Strand, London WC2R 0RL, England

First published in the United States of America by Dutton Books,

a member of Penguin Group (USA) Inc., 2011

Published by Speak, an imprint of Penguin Group (USA) Inc., 2012

This book is a work of fiction. Names, characters, places, and incidents are either the product of the author's imagination or are used fictitiously, and any resemblance to actual persons, living or dead, business establishments, events, or locales is entirely coincidental.

1 3 5 7 9 10 8 6 4 2

THE LIBRARY OF CONGRESS HAS CATALOGED THE DUTTON BOOKS EDITION AS FOLLOWS:

Scott, Elizabeth, date.

As I wake / by Elizabeth Scott. – 1st ed.

p. cm.

Summary: Seventeen-year-old Ava awakens with amnesia and a feeling that something is wrong with her life, her mother, and her friends but when the mysterious Morgan appears, her flashbacks of life as a spy for a shady government agency begin to make sense.

ISBN: 978-0-525-42209-9 (hc)

[1. Supernatural—Fiction. 2. Identity—Fiction. 3. Mothers and daughters—Fiction. 4. Love—Fiction. 5. Memory—Fiction.]

I. Title.

PZ7.S4195As 2011

[Fic]—dc22   2011005198

Speak ISBN 978-0-14-242246-5

Designed by Irene Vandervoort
Type set in Bell

Printed in the United States of America

For Jess,
because she always believed in this story,
and helped me to keep believing too

as i wake

1.

WAKE UP.

I'm in bed. Sheets and blankets tucked around me, my legs sprawled out like I've fallen. No light in the room except faint yellow and a darker, colder gleam shining through the window, its curtains only partly closed.

Where am I?

I don't know these sheets, this bed, this room.

I look down at myself, see soft fabric wrapping me from neck to knees. My feet are bare.

There are dark shapes all around.

People?

I slide up onto my elbows slowly, creeping back until my shoulders hit the wooden back of the bed. I sit quiet, watching. Waiting.

No movement. No breathing other than my own.

There are no people here, just things. Chair. Dresser. Desk. Lamp. I can see them as my eyes adjust to the dark. Familiar shapes, words easy on my tongue but still—

I don't recognize these dark shapes, these things.

Where am I?

I get up.

The door to the room I'm in opens easily, unlocked, swinging free, and I step into a hall. It's dark and there is carpet under my feet, thick and soft. It extends out past me, leads to two closed doors.

What hides behind them?

I don't want to look.

Stairs. I see them now, a little to my left, and move toward them, grateful. I do not know where they lead, but it has to be away and that—that is better than those closed doors.

The stairs are carpeted too, soft under my feet, and down and down and down I walk into more darkness.

I can walk. I can talk, whisper "carpet" into the dark. I know words: hands, door, nightgown, bed, dark, light.

Where am I?

Bottom of the stairs, wood under my feet now, I'm standing on a floor, darkness all around edged only by the deeper darkness of more rooms, waiting shadows.

Door to my left, just a few steps away.

I move toward it carefully, my feet silently crossing

the floor. I see my toes, but they do not feel like mine. I am dreaming maybe, one where everything is familiar but not, understood but not known.

I open the door.

Night, it is night, and a streetlight glows strong enough that it bleeds across the faint light of stars that strain above it.

Close my eyes.

I think about stars. Their light comes from years beyond years away. Constellations: Big Dipper, Orion. Venus sometimes shines brightly, low in the night sky, and is mistaken for a star.

I open my eyes.

I still don't know here. Don't know this place.

Where am I?

There are more stairs, rugged for outside, for weather, and I walk down them. I walk away from the room, the hall, the stairs.

I turn around, see a tall shape, boxy dark in the night.

A house.

I don't know it.

Where am I?

I back away, step onto grass. It's cold and wet

against my feet, sends a chill crawling through my toes and up my spine.

Walking, I am walking, almost running, off the grass and onto a road, the streetlight beaming at the end of it, glowing over a sign. Homeway Lane.

Where am I?

Street, alley, driveway, walk, road, I know.

I don't know Homeway Lane.

Where am I?

Close my eyes, this is just a dream, a weird, bad dream, like—

I don't know.

I don't know any of my bad dreams. I don't know—

I open my eyes.

It's still dark, still night, my skin is cold and I have goose bumps, but this isn't real, it's just a dream, a bad dream, and I know that just like I know that I am—I am—I am—

I don't know.

I don't know.

Close eyes, shaking now. End dream.

2.

WAKE UP.

OhGodOhGodOhGodOhGod someone says, arms around me, holding tight.

I struggle, push.

I get some space, and then flinch away from the woman looking at me. I don't know the wide, scared eyes, the shiny nose, the shaking mouth.

I don't know her.

OhGodOhGodOhGod she says. Her voice matches her eyes, high-pitched and terrified.

"Ma'am, you need to let go of her. We have to look at her," another voice says. Deeper voice, a guy whose face is broken up by the flashing lights of the ambulance behind him.

The streetlight is still on. Still shining on the sign. Homeway Lane.

"No," I say, but nothing changes. I don't wake up.

I don't know where I am.

I don't know who I am.

A light shines in my eyes and behind it I see the

shadow of a face, dark eyes staring sadly, wearily into mine. (How do I see all this and not know where I am? How do I not know who I am?)

Close my eyes. Wake up, wake up, this is all a dream.

"Looks like she's high," the man with the weary eyes says, and then leans into me, forcing my eyes up, shining bright light into me so I can't sleep. Can't get away.

"What did you take?" he says into my ear, taking his time with each word, as if it has to fly to me from somewhere far away. "Your mother says you've been home all night but—"

Mother? The word makes my heart pound faster, ticktock shattering in my chest. "Mother?"

He blinks at the way I say the word, then gestures at the OhGod woman, who is huddled nearby, staring at me. Her eyes are full of want and pleading, and her hands are reaching for me.

"I don't know her," I say, moving away even though her fingers can't quite touch me, and the woman's mouth falls open.

"You have to take her to the hospital," she says, and then does reach me, moves and grabs my arm, fingers sliding around my wrist, clinging tight. "Ava, honey, we have to go to the hospital now, okay? You'll be fine, though. You're going to be fine."

Ava?

"Is that your name?" the man with the light says, arms folding me onto a stretcher, twirling this place around me, Homeway Lane turning out of sight, and the woman looks at me like she knows me. Looks so happy.

This is a dream; this has to be a dream.

"Ava, can you hear me?" the man says, and I don't want to be pushed down onto a stretcher. I don't want this, I want to go, I want to wake up but I'm not, I'm not, and I can't breathe, there isn't enough air in me, in this place and the OhGod woman is still here, still looking at me, and she looks so real, all this looks so real, and I just want to go to sleep, I just want to wake up and breathe, stop this heavy fuzzy darkness in my head.

Shock, I hear someone say as the darkness starts to swallow me, creeping up all around. Oh shit, she's going into shock.

I close my eyes.

3.

I LOOK AROUND THE ATTIC. *I don't need to, of course. I know it, I've seen the plans for the whole building, memorized them. I learned how to do that early on when I was in school, hoping that I'd be here, that I'd be part of SAT, the State Antiterrorism Taskforce. It's cold, but after I've been here for a while my body heat will warm the air, stop my breath from coming out in frosty puffs.*

I stroke the side of the chair I'm sitting on, my fingers skating over the cracked orange plastic, and turn on the headset.

I am here, finally, and I must do a good job. I know what will happen if I am lazy or sloppy or stupid. The People's Democratic Movement, the ones who make the rules that keep us safe, who run everything, who want to know everything—they will know if I fail. They know everything.

And if I do, the crèche will swallow me again, that I will disappear inside its endless gray walls full of children who are unwanted, or, like I was, orphaned and watched, doomed to nothingness unless they can prove themselves. The PDM is letting me try, letting me be part of something

*that is as necessary as breathing, for if the SAT isn't work-
ing, if people aren't looking out for each other, listening or
watching or doing whatever it takes to keep everyone safe,
then we aren't part of a strong government. We'd be at the
mercy of anyone who wanted anything.*

If we have all the information, no one can ever hurt us.

*There are no instructions for me to read, but I don't
need them. I was trained for this. I've proved myself. I can
do this in my sleep. Power on listening device, switch on
right side; hit pause to show start of duty, and then begin
recording. Extra batteries are stored inside the bottom of
the unit, and all battery changes must be done after noting
them in my report.*

*I unfold the keyboard. It is sticky. The other person who
listens here, the silent man who left when I came in, must
have eaten. My stomach rumbles. He must be higher in the
SAT than I am.*

*Of course he is. He didn't come from the crèche, isn't a
child of those who did things that SAT works to stop.*

*I open the report. The date and time fill themselves in
automatically, and the field for subject is labeled "56-412.
MORGAN." It doesn't say why 56-412 is being watched.*

*There is no need to. Everyone who might matter, who
might possibly think things that could hurt the government,*

is watched at one time or another. That is what the SAT does, and this is just 56-412's time. It might just be a few days. It might be a few months.

Or 56-412 might say something that could harm the PDM, in which case he'll disappear and I—

I will have another job. I've proven myself. I have.

I listen, hands hovering over the keys.

After a moment, I type 56-412, Sleeping. It is the same as the last entry, and the one before it.

56-412 rolls over. I hear the bed rustling, and curl my feet into my socks, wishing I had better shoes.

56-412 breathes slowly, deeply. I try breathing like that too. The best way to understand those who might want to harm the state is to know them, to do what I am doing now, to listen and serve the greater good, but after a few minutes I feel myself sliding toward sleep. I stayed up too late last night waiting for now, waiting for my life to truly begin.

I close my eyes.

4.

WAKE UP.

I see white-green lights flickering overhead. I'm flat
on my back, a bed under me and a television high up on
the wall, its screen dark. White walls, and signs at eye
level: NO PHONES, NO ELECTRONIC DEVICES, NO SMOKING,
PLEASE STOP AT THE DESK BEFORE LEAVING THE HOSPITAL.

Hospital. I'm in the hospital. I must have been in
an accident. I try to remember it, but my head hurts,
blinding hot pain, and I squeeze my eyes shut, see an
attic, an orange chair, and the number 56-412.

The pain gets worse, and I push the images away,
see a house and a road and a streetlight shining down
on me.

Which one is real? I have to think.

Go on, do it. I'll tell myself to.

_____, think.

What? No. no no no no.

_____, think.

I feel myself start to shake.

I don't know who I am. My head aches and is

empty, full of words but nothing more. I sit up, frantic, scrabbling at the bed, at my body (Is it real? Is any of this real?), and startle a slumped lump in a chair in the corner.

One look shows me it's the woman from before, from the street. The house.

The one who says she's my mother.

"Ava, honey," she says, and is there, right there, grabbing me again, covering one of my hands with her own. Her skin is warm, normal.

Real.

Skin renews itself daily, new cells born, old cells die. The human body is a complex machine, and there is one spot on the foot that, if pressed, will make your body cramp in pain. People will answer questions if you place your fingers there and push.

I know that, but I do not know this woman.

I do not know me.

"Ava?" the woman says again, and I look at her for a moment. Her eyes are scared but happy too, and she keeps patting my hand. I crawl my fingers away.

Her face falls, going sad.

"Honey, it's me, it's okay," she says, as if that means everything.

It means nothing and I swing my legs away from her, my feet on the floor. I still don't have shoes, and the floor is cold.

The door opens and a man—a doctor, I know from the way he walks, the way he's dressed—comes in and looks at me.

"So you woke up," he says, and I stare at him because this has to be a dream. Doctors never come to a hospital room unless something very bad has happened because there simply aren't enough of them. The study required—and the screening for it—is intense, and few meet the qualifications of intellect and respect for all that's done to keep us all safe.

"I—I think I'm still asleep," I say, and he frowns, looking at the not-mother.

"No, you're awake," he says, moving toward me as a nurse comes in behind him, head bowed over a tray she's holding. "You hyperventilated on the way here and passed out, and then you did seem to fall asleep for a while. How are you feeling now?"

"You don't—I know something's wrong," I say. "You wouldn't—you wouldn't be here if there wasn't. And the attic and the orange chair and the number—" I break off, my head hurting again, sudden cramping pain, and know—yes, know—that I shouldn't say any more. That I must be careful.

The doctor frowns, and then looks at the chair the not-mother was sitting in.

Orange plastic.

Then he touches my wrist once, gently and impersonally as the nurse moves around behind me. I look down, see what he sees, thin strip of plastic around my wrist.

Ava Hanson, it says. Allergies, none. 56-412.

"I don't—I thought—" I say, and the woman who called me Ava, the mother not-mother, says, "Oh, honey," and starts to cry, big wet tears and hiccuping sobs.

"Mrs. Hanson," the doctor says, and the woman shakes her head, says, "I'm sorry," and moves away.

Her eyes are full of pain.

5.

THE DOCTOR ASKS ME where I live. "Your address," he says, when I don't answer.

"I don't know."

"What were you doing tonight before your mother found you?"

I force my body to go rigid, to not shake. I force myself to look into the endless dark of my brain and search. "I don't know."

He looks at Mrs. Hanson and I keep trying, looking for something, but there is only blankness because behind the bed and the light, behind Homeway Lane, there is nothing, and all I think when I think "Me" is—

Nothing. I am a blank, a blur.

"Okay. Tell me exactly what you do remember," the doctor says.

"Double-checking temperature," the nurse says, moving around the doctor to scan my forehead with a small plastic machine.

"I woke up in a room and I didn't—I didn't know where I was. So I left and I went downstairs, I went outside—"

"See, she knows the house," Mrs. Hanson says. "She knows how to go downstairs, and she knew how to open the front door. She's fine. I'm sure she's fine. She has to be—"

"Mrs. Hanson," the doctor says, so kindly, so evenly, and so full of pity that my skin prickles, and then he turns back to me and says, "Where are we?"

"The hospital."

"And where is the hospital?"

I stare at him because I don't know.

I know what a hospital is, I know what this room means, but it could be anywhere, I could be anywhere, and I don't know how I woke up in that house or who Ava Hanson is and who her mother is and why I'm here, why I'm supposed to be here.

The doctor frowns a little and then looks at Mrs. Hanson, the mother who has claimed me. "We'll need to run some tests."

"Temperature's normal," the nurse says, and when I look at her she is blurred around the edges somehow, as if she's here but not here, but then she becomes clear and I see an old woman, grandmother-age with silver hair and hands so thin they are nothing but knotty ropes of veins, watching me, dressed all in white like an angel.

She is smiling at me, but her smile is like broken glass, shiny and sharp.

She knows things about me. I can see it, and for the first time since this dream that won't end began, I know something too. I know she has answers.

"Where am I?" I say. "Who am I?"

She points at the plastic on my wrist and says, "Hospital, of course. But soon you'll be back home. Be back to your old self. You'll see."

"But I—" I say and then stop because she puts her fingers on my wrist and her skin is cold like winter, like her eyes, and I'm not sure what I'm seeing now. I thought she knew things but my head is spinning, painful but not, like it is being looked at from the inside, and—

"Ava," the doctor says, and I blink, see him frowning at me. The nurse has two fingers on the inside of my wrist still, frowning as her eyes squint in concentration. She looks different though, younger.

"What happened to the other nurse?" I say, and she looks at the doctor.

"There was no other nurse," he says, and then looks at Ava's mother. "She drifted away just now, somehow. Her eyes were open, even. We have to run more tests."

"But she—she's here, she's going to be all right," Ava's mother says, her voice rising. "You don't understand, but if I could just take her home—"

There is more talking, lots of it, but this isn't real, it can't be, I can't be a blank, unknown and full of darkness. And then I am being gently pushed onto the bed again, the ceiling gleaming down at me, and I don't know this place but the older nurse knew something, knows me. I remember that. I know it.

She said I was going home soon and so I will because I will wake up. I will. I have to.

I close my eyes.

Nothing happens.

I just see dark edged with light, sneaking in and flickering green-white while Ava's mother cries and the doctor talks more about tests and the nurse, the young one, the one who wasn't here before, says, "I'll go see if the neurologist is here yet."

I close my eyes tighter but nothing happens. I don't wake up.

When I finally open them Ava's mother is looking down at me.

"Everything will be fine," she says. "Really, honey, it will," and the doctor says, "Yes, it will," and I don't know where I am. I don't know who I am.

But I know a lie when I hear one.

6.

56-412 SLEEPS. *56-412 wakes up. I hear it; the stirring, the shifting of arms and legs, the scissoring up from dreams.*

56-412 listens to music. I force my feet to stay still, to not tap along because music doesn't benefit anyone. It's hard, though, because I've only heard the national anthem and it doesn't beat in a way that snakes inside you.

56-412's phone rings, and the music stops. 56-412 is quiet, but doesn't answer the phone.

I listen, I hear the sounds of breathing. In, out, in, out. The phone rings and rings and rings. Why won't he answer the phone? I can't believe he has one. The waiting list for one is years. Usually only PDM officials or their families can get one.

Breathing is regulated by the central nervous system. It happens without thought.

My feet are cold. I think of shoes, lined with warm fabric. If I do well, if I get permission to shop in a government store, an official store, I can buy some. One day, I might even be able to get on the line for a phone, although if I talk on it someone like me will listen to every word I say. The SAT is always, always vigilant. That was the first thing I learned. We have to keep everyone safe, and everyone has a part to play in that—unless they are trying to hurt the PDM. Hurt us.

I yawn, rest my head on my hand. Tell myself to keep listening, to stay awake. To wait. Something will happen. I know it.

I can feel it.

7.

I WAKE UP SCREAMING.

I wake up inside a machine. I can't see anything, I'm in a tube and its insides are pressed up against me and the noise, so much noise, a harsh rhythmic clanging. I've dreamed myself inside a grave, I've dreamed myself dead, and I scream and scream and scream.

I've fallen asleep inside an MRI machine. The doctors—I have more now—tell me that. They are looking inside my head.

They give me something to make me sleep; they have to run these tests and no, there aren't any phones ringing, they say when I ask. I see them look at each other.

I see Ava's mother watching me, hands held out like she's waiting for me to take them before I close my eyes.

8.

WAKE UP.

I am still in the hospital. Still in a world where everything is a blank.

But there is a reason for the blankness, for all my confusion.

I have amnesia.

I have forgotten myself. The doctors think I might have gotten an infection inside my head, all around my brain, and that's what made my memory go away.

There was no trace of an infection in any of the tests they say, but I'm young and healthy and probably fought it off without ever feeling bad.

I just lost my memory instead.

I don't see the gray-haired nurse again, but she's right, I get to go home.

Sort of.

I'm sent away from the hospital, told I'm young and healthy, I'm lucky. I'm told, "Ava, you're a lucky girl; things could have been much worse; you'll get everything back; you'll be fine. Take care."

It's repeated over and over, a song of words, until I find myself outside the hospital, inside a car I don't know—brown on the outside, brown on the inside, stranger mother, Ava's mother, asking me if I'm hungry or thirsty or need anything as we drive down streets I don't know back to a house I do because I'd woken up in it and thought I was dreaming.

But I wasn't.

It's where I'm supposed to be.

9.

AVA HANSON is seventeen. She is a junior at
Lakewood Day, which is a private school and expensive,
but worth it because Jane, Ava's mother, wants Ava to
get the best education she can, and Ava likes Lakewood
Day. Loves it, even. She writes in a messy scrawl, her *A*
huge and the rest of her name almost hidden inside it.

My handwriting matches hers.

Ava has always lived with her mother. Her father
died before she was born.

There are pictures of Ava and her mother. Jane
shows them to me, shows them all to me, and I watch
Ava go from tiny to tall, up and up until Ava stands
looking down at her mother, half grin/half scowl on
her face.

I can twist my mouth the same way.

I look like the girl in the photos.

I don't remember anything.

Inside my head is empty space. I know things; every-
day life things, and a few things that make Jane's eyes

shade strange, afraid when I mention them ("Crèche?"
she says when I ask. "No, Ava, honey, you were never in
one of those. I don't even know what that is!")

I feel things too; hunger and sleepiness and boredom
(I don't care about Ava's first grade report cards)—and
fear.

Fear is always with me.

I should remember things. This. Me. (Shouldn't I?)

But I don't.

10.

ON MY FIFTH DAY of being Ava, I get up early. I am not sleeping well, and when I do, I dream of the orange chair I saw when I thought I'd woken up but hadn't.

I dream of it, and the attic. Of listening to 56-412 sleep.

My hospital bracelet sits on my dresser. The numbers on it are not 56-412; they are longer, my social security number. I asked about seeing 56-412 but was told I was tired, that stress was making my condition worse. The same thing had happened with the nurse I thought I saw, remember?

Yes, that I did.

I was told not to worry, that things would be better soon, I'd remember everything.

I get up, silent so I can slip away from Jane. From her need, her longing for her daughter. Her Ava.

I walk outside, and the road looks just like it did the night I woke up wondering where and who I was, dark. I walk away from the sign I don't know, from Homeway Lane, walk up the road.

Little bits of rock and grit crunch into my feet. Ava seems to love shoes and has twenty pairs, but all of them have heels that make my ankles wobble when I put them on and so I am barefoot, my feet on the ground connecting me to the earth.

I need that.

I look down at the ground and close my eyes.

After a moment I open them. I see my bare toes on the road. I am here.

I am not dreaming. This is me. This is my life.

But it doesn't feel right.

It doesn't feel like mine, it still feels like a dream I'm in, that I've been put in.

I shake my head, so confused, and when I look up, my heart-stutter stops, my breath freezing.

The older nurse from the hospital is on the road too, walking toward me, her gray hair haloed by the rising sun. She reaches me easily, walking with long, strong strides. Her shoes are gray like her hair, and crunch into the grit and rocks, crushing them. Her smile is like snow, beautiful and cold.

"Well, hello there," she says. "I see you're out of the hospital."

She will not pretend, then. Good.

"I saw you there."

"Well, I would think so," she says. "I volunteer there, you know. Take people to visit their relatives, walk them to where they need to go, that sort of thing."

"You told me I was going home," I say, and she smiles at me again, her teeth glittering white.

My head hurts, sudden and vicious pain, again like the inside of my mind is being squeezed. Rearranged. *I see a face leaning over me, and the smile, I know the smile, I know—*

"I don't remember saying that," she says, and puts one hand on my arm. "You don't look well, Ava. Maybe you're—well, maybe you need to relax. Enjoy your life and not worry about remembering it."

I remember her hand.

I **know** her hand.

"You—I—you were there, you told me I was going home but you—" I say, and then gasp, the pain in the my head doubling, tripling, turning her into two old ladies, both of them staring at me, both of them watching me, unblinking. One watching me in the dark. One in the light. That smile. Her hands.

How can there be two of her?

How can I see them both?

"Careful, Ava," she says, and steers me, her hand
guiding me, pushing me along, and twigs grab at my
skin, pinching it, the smell of forest all around me.

I don't see woods, just the road, the streetlight, and
the sign, but when I move I have to push the twigs
away, push away from the woods—

And there is nothing there, I am touching nothing,
and my insides twist like I am going to throw up.

"Ava," I gasp, and she stops, looks at me.

"We really need to get you home, I think," she says,
and I shake my head, agony because of the pain, a tight
squeezing band that throbs from the top of my scalp to
the very edge of my jaw.

It's like a knife inside me but it doesn't stop what
I see.

What I know.

I know a world but it's not this one, I know I don't
belong here.

I know something else too.

"You know my name. You know I'm Ava," I say, and
her eyes go sharp like her smile but she isn't smiling
now, isn't smiling at all, but only says, "Well, of course
I know," in a patient way, as if I have said something
silly, and then waves one arm in the air like a signal.

— 3 2 —

But I haven't said something silly. She knows who I am. She says *Ava* and I know it. I feel it.

I remember it as my name. *My* name.

And I've heard her say it before.

I try to say something else but the pain in my head gets worse, forcing me to my knees, and I hear the old lady call out "Jane, over here," and then Ava's mom is running toward us, I know the way her feet sound, it's all I've heard for days, and then she is here, grabbing my other arm and saying, "Ava? Ava?"

And then I throw up all over the old lady's shoes.

"Migraine," the old lady says, and smiles—warm this time, gentle, even—at Jane, who has pulled me to her, holding me up.

"Clementine, I didn't know you lived around here," she says, her voice shaking.

"Oh, I was just out for my morning walk," the old lady, Clementine, says. "It's good to exercise, you know. Do you still walk, Jane?"

"I've been busy lately," Jane says, and her voice is stronger now. Sharper. "I—well, you can see Ava isn't quite herself."

"Oh, she'll be all right," Clementine says. "After all, she has her mother to take care of her, doesn't she?"

"Yes," Jane says, and that one word is full of a million things, all of them compressed together and too big for me to understand, and I force myself to stand up, ready to walk away with Jane, but she doesn't move. She stands there, watching Clementine, who glances down at her shoes, sighs, and then strides briskly away.

She doesn't look back.

"Do you— Do you want to go back to your—the house?" I say after a moment. The pain in my head is letting up a little, the pressure easing into a dull throb.

I think about Clementine, about how she knew me—knows me—and how my name sounded so right, so true when she said it, and the pain comes back.

I gasp, fighting it, and I see . . .

I see myself, sitting down at a desk taking notes as everyone around me whispers her name. "You know what Clementine did to her own child?" "Well, her family were traitors, and the PDM has to keep us all safe. She did the right thing." "I heard they moved her from SAT to the Science Labs but she still has ties to SAT, and—"

I dry heave, snapping back to Jane as she says, "Oh, Ava, honey, I'm sorry," and wraps one arm around me, helping me down the road. Helping me back to the house.

"How do you know Clementine?" I say when Jane has walked me upstairs and to Ava's room and tucked me into Ava's bed.

"You need to get some sleep," she says. "And I'm going to call your doctors. You—you shouldn't be like this. In pain."

She hasn't answered my question. I look at her, and she stares back at me, worry creasing her face.

"I don't know her, not really," Jane says. "I see her out walking sometimes, that's all."

"But she knows me, and I know her."

"No, that's not possible," Jane says, her voice firm. "I've never seen you talk to her before today. She's a little old to be a friend of yours, after all." Then she kisses my forehead and tells me to rest, that she'll check on me soon.

When I am alone I think about Clementine's smile and how I don't want to know it. But I do. I know I do.

The Ava I'm supposed to be doesn't know her.

But the Ava I am does.

I am here, in this world, in this life.

But I don't think I'm from here.

I don't think I belong here.

I close my eyes.

11.

56-412 *is eating noodles. I hear the slurping sound that everyone makes when they eat them and my stomach cramps because I haven't eaten since before I came here and it was only toast, the heel of an old loaf that hurt my teeth when I chewed.*

56-412 lets out a sigh and stands up. His chair scrapes across the floor. I listen, wondering what he will do now, but hear nothing.

Three days here, in this attic, in this chair, and there's been nothing but reading and sleeping and eating and showering and one phone call that wasn't answered—the intercept never clicked on.

I wish his life was mine.

I look around then, guiltily, as if someone can hear me. You never know, and I even check my mouth to make sure it is closed. It is, of course. I know what words can do. I am here because of them, am hear to listen, to make sure the wrong ones aren't said. I don't know why 56-412 is being watched. His file is very thin, like he just appeared a few years ago. That shouldn't be possible but with all the files SAT has, sometimes things get lost in the PDM archives.

I wish my file had gotten lost.

Still nothing from 56-412. Must be sleeping . . . no. He's reading again. I hear the slow flip of pages turning. I sigh and close my eyes.

12.

WAKE UP.

I'm not in a chair, I'm in a bed. Ava's bed.

I was dreaming again. I wonder why I dream the same, about the attic and the chair and the numbers. The person I never see, but listen to.

I wonder why it feels so much more real than this. Than me, here, in this room.

Because it was real.

If it was real, then how did I get here? Why am I here? I close my eyes again.

It takes me a long time to sleep and when I do, no dreams come.

13.

AFTER A WEEK OF AVA STORIES and Ava
pictures and Ava, Ava, Ava, Jane tells me she has to go
back to work. She says it as we're eating dinner—pizza
with pepperoni and olives.

Jane doesn't like to cook much and besides, Ava
loves pizza, loves olives. I like them both too and I am
so desperate for something, anything to make sense, to
feel real, to make me believe I am someone, that I am
a me and not just a question mark, so I smile and Jane
smiles back. It is so easy to make her happy.

"So, we have options," Jane says. "You can try going
back to school, or I can—well, there's a group of doctors at the university hospital, and they'd be interested
in seeing you."

"All the time? Instead of school?"

Jane looks at her pizza. "It's a neurology lab, and
they're very interested in trying to get a grant to study
how memory works and they . . . they think you would
be helpful to them. That they could help you remember
who you are."

I feel myself relax, an unconscious effort my body seems to know how to do even though my mind is racing and I feel anything but relaxed. I don't know anything about me, but my body knows things. It is good at pretending. At smiling, at looking calm.

At lying.

"Help me how?"

"Well, there'd be tests," Jane says. "If you're interested, I'll arrange for us to go in and talk to them."

Testing. I remember that, remember the doctors and their machines and their needles poking me, testing me, drawing my blood and all saying everything will be fine, you'll be fine, as if not knowing who I am is nothing.

As if they wanted me gone because they couldn't fix me. They couldn't even find where things went wrong. They looked at every part of me and all they could conclude was what I'd known from the moment I woke up.

I don't know this place. I don't know me.

I don't think I can.

The Ava I am isn't the Ava I'm supposed to be.

I just don't know why I'm here. Why I'm her.

"School," I say. "I'll go to school."

"Good," Jane says, and grins at me. "I know the

hospital was . . . it was hard for me to see you like that and I don't . . . I don't want that to happen again. And I think getting back to normal will be good. It'll help you. Plus Sophy and Greer and Olivia have all called for you, so I know they want to see you."

"Who?"

She blinks, then says, "Your friends," putting her piece of pizza down on her plate and then pushing it away.

It takes her a moment to speak again, and when she does, her voice is very soft. Very eager. Very nervous. "Ava, do you—do you remember anything yet?"

I don't know Jane, but her longing for her daughter gets to me, slides under the worry that coats me.

"Olives," I say, and she smiles wide and brilliant, like everything is okay, but that night, as I am sitting on the floor of Ava's room, awake again and looking into the dark, I hear her crying.

I move over to the window and push the curtain aside. Up past the broad glare glow of the streetlight, the stars shine faintly, tiny blurs of light. I see the Big Dipper and trace its shapes across the glass with one finger.

I hear Jane get up. I hear her get out of bed, pad

out into the hall. I dive back into Ava's bed, pulling the covers across myself, and close my eyes as my door opens and she looks in at me.

She goes downstairs and walks around for a while, footsteps tracing from the kitchen to the front door, the door I went out of that first night, and back again. Then there is silence, followed by a faint tapping noise. She's on the phone. Jane always taps a pen against something when she's on the phone.

I don't remember her, but I am starting to know her. There is a strange sort of comfort in that.

Whoever she's talking to must make her upset because her voice rises to a level I can hear and she says, "You didn't tell me it would be like this. You said she'd be—hello? Hello? Damn!"

Then she cries.

I listen. Her tears sound like me, lost and scared, and I get up and go downstairs, go to her.

"Ava, honey," she says, seeing me and wiping her eyes. "What are you doing up?"

I look at the phone, then back at her. Her gaze skitters away from mine, nervous.

We all have secrets. I wonder what Jane's are.

I know I can find out. Not memory, something

deeper, stronger. Something me. Something that knows I can gain trust. Find answers.

I smile at her. "I can't sleep."

"Me either," she says, and glances at the phone, a fast, frightened look. "I guess you going back to school has got me thinking . . . do you want to look at some photos again? I could make popcorn."

"Sure," I say, and so I listen to her tell me stories about photos I have seen but still don't know, listen to her tell me about Ava's life and school.

All mine, now.

"I like your shirt," I say, pointing at the last picture where a girl who looks like me is frowning, arms crossed over her chest as Jane grins at the camera against a backdrop of beach.

"You gave it to me for my birthday," she says, and puts one arm around me.

It doesn't feel familiar, but it doesn't feel wrong either, and when I don't move away her smile is so full, so strong, that I want to remember Ava for her. It would make her so happy, and I think it would be easy to be her daughter.

I could maybe become the Ava she wants me to be.

14.

AVA WEARS a lot of black. Her closet is full of it, and I go to school in black jeans and a black shirt with black boots whose tall, pointy heels make my ankles feel wobbly. I don't like the clothes, but Jane is happy to see me in them, says, "Ava, honey, you look—you look like you! I guess you'll blend right back in, won't you?"

Blend in? If Ava wanted to blend in, she should wear brown and gray and shoes that don't have heels that make sharp clipped noises every time I take a step. Also, her bag is covered with scrawled words like *PEACE* and *HATE* and *LOVE* and *FUDGE!* written in bright colors. It looks messy and screams "Look At Me!"

"I don't want to take this," I say, because I don't. I don't want carry it; I don't even like it.

Jane looks surprised, but happy, and says, "Are you sure?"

When I nod she goes into her room and comes back with a simple gray bag. "I kept this after we went shopping before last term, hoping you'd—well, I guess for once we agree on something you're wearing."

"You don't like my clothes?"

"Oh no, no, I—I know you like them," she says.

"But I don't."

"You don't?" she says, and when I nod her eyes widen, hope gathering, and she says, "Maybe you—do you feel something when you put them on?"

More distance from who I'm supposed to be. And also, my feet hurt. "Like what?"

"Like—upset, maybe?" she says, and I realize she sees something in these clothes, sees her own memories in them and that something—whatever led me here—is tied up in an Ava she hasn't told me about. One who dresses in clothes Jane doesn't like.

Who goes to school and lives a life that Jane could know nothing about.

My head starts to hurt.

"No, nothing like that," I mumble, and when she asks me if I'm fine I say Yes and Yes again and then "YES, I said YES okay?" when she asks for the third time and she flinches, but then smiles so bright and says, "That's my girl," happy and scared-sounding all at once and I realize she's told me nothing but happy stories, that all I know is that Jane loves Ava and Ava loves Jane, but that can't be all because even happiness has its tiny bits of bitter in it.

I don't know how I know that, but I do. I can feel the beat of that truth inside me. Taste it bitter on my tongue.

Sometimes, like now, I don't think I want to know who I really am.

15.

LAKEWOOD DAY is a series of light-colored buildings smoothed together in a circle and surrounded by neatly trimmed grass and small areas where flowers and neatly trimmed trees bloom, decorated with people standing, sitting, slouching.

All of them are talking and as Jane asks if she should come in with me, question filled with hope in her voice, I can't do anything but stare.

Everyone seems so . . . I don't know. Full of energy but not on edge. Ready, but not suspicious. There is ease here, there is hope and fear and lust and anger, every emotion, and so thick I can almost smell them, but one thing is absent.

Fear.

I hadn't known I'd expected it until now, and without it, I feel . . . lost.

I don't understand these people.

I want Jane to come with me, to be watched like the few adults I see are, to give me time to think, to understand why here, why school—and I do know that word, I do—seems so wrong.

A place so not what I understand in a place beyond memory, in a place I can't reach but can feel.

I turn to her, but before I can speak there is knocking on the car window, not hard but eager, and I hear voices saying, "Ava!!"

"Hi, girls," Jane says, rolling down the window and I inhale perfume and am enveloped in black-clad arms, in voices saying my name and greeting Jane, in the smell of perfume and hair; black, brown, and a shade in between, that wraps around me too.

And that's how I meet Greer, Olivia, and Sophy. Ava's friends.

There is more hugging as I get out of the car, hands moving away from me to wave at Jane as she drives away, and then they all step back, look at me.

"So?" one says, short but unquestionably the leader, the other two standing slightly behind her and watching her as much as they watch me. Her hair is long and black, her clothes are even more attention-calling than mine, layers upon layers of floaty, filmy black that complement her hair.

She bites her nails, though. Bites them right down to the skin. She is a leader who lives with fear.

"Hi, Sophy, Olivia, Greer," I say, and the black-haired girl says, "See? I told you guys she'd remember us," and then hugs me again. "Tell Olivia she owes me twenty bucks."

I look at the other two girls. One is the first girl's height, and has a heart-shaped face with curls ringing it. The other is taller, and seems as awkward in her all-black outfit as I feel, is looking at people walking by and watching us as she picks at the hem of her long black shirt. Her hair is straight and shiny, a dark brown that is too dull to be black, and her eyes, when they meet mine, are cool. Assessing.

"I don't know who Olivia is," I say, and meet the eyes of the girl with the straight hair. The one who is watching me intently. She doesn't bite her nails at all, and she doesn't blink when I look at her.

She should be the leader of this little group, but she isn't.

"Told you, Greer," the girl with heart-shaped face says, and gives me a blinding, silly happy smile that she turns on the leader. "Now you owe me."

"No way, Olivia," Greer says, smoothing her black hair back behind her ears. "She said our names. That counts." She grins at me, open and sunny, but with a hint of warning.

It doesn't bother me. I know her warning is something I can handle easily, that it is nothing but surface show—and wonder again who the Ava I'm supposed to be is.

"So, how did you know it was us?" the tallest one, the watchful one, Sophy, says, her voice quieter than I think she wants it to be.

"The clothes," I say, watching her face. "We all look . . ."

"Totally unique, I know," Greer says, and smiles at me for real. "We aren't slaves to the stupid mall like some people."

"Totally unique," Olivia echoes. Her clothes are a match for Greer's but catch on her curves. Of all the people who walk by and stare—and most of them do, sigh-sneering at the clothes, and then eyes widening at me—the guys always watch Olivia.

She's looking at Greer, though, and doesn't seem to notice.

A bell rings, loud and jarring, and a universal groan seems to echo out. I see a few instructors, standing in their classroom doorways, but they don't look angered by the noise, just resigned.

"Do you remember your schedule?" Greer asks, tapping my arm when I don't look at her right away. "What are you staring at?"

"No one's in trouble for not wanting to go to class?"

Greer laughs. "If we got in trouble for that, there'd be maybe three students here. You have forgotten everything, haven't you?"

She shakes her head at me, then says, "Don't worry, I still love you," and strides off into the crowd. Olivia plunges after her, but not before pressing a piece of paper into my hand and saying, "Here. I wrote down all your classes for you. My mom read this book on brain injuries last year and talked about it forever, so I figured that you might, you know, need help and—" She breaks off as Greer comes back.

"Are you coming?" she says to Olivia, and then looks at me and Sophy and says, "Ditch third, okay?"

"Oh, I forgot to tell you about that," Olivia says, but Greer says, "Olivia, are we going now or what?" and

Olivia gives me another quick smile and follows Greer, the two of them vanishing into the sea of people moving around us.

"So, see you later," Sophy says. "You sure you're going to be able to find your classes and stuff?" She doesn't say what ditching third is, and I know she won't.

"I'm fine," I say, and when Sophy smiles at my answer, my lie, her smile doesn't reach her eyes.

I feel a chill crawl through me because Sophy's smile that isn't one?

I know it.

16.

I'M EXHAUSTED by the time I'm in what I think is fourth period, confused by the hallways, by the way everyone I pass is so vibrant, so alive with their endless parade of clothes that look the same but have individual touches. Even if I wore the clothes everyone else has, I wouldn't be able to make them my own like they can.

There's nothing in me—no me—to draw on.

The teacher talks about government, and how it's structured. I don't understand any of it, and the notebooks I found in Ava's locker (combination on the paper Olivia gave me) are empty except for tiny, simple drawings, boxes and squiggles, and the name Ethan, tucked into the corner of most pages. I write my own Ethan next to one of Ava's.

They look exactly alike.

It's warm in the classroom, so warm I feel my tense—very tense—body, relax a little, and the teacher is talking and talking. I rest my head on one hand and yawn.

17.

MY JAW CRACKS *and I sit up straighter, ashamed of myself for almost falling asleep.*

At least I'm not in school anymore. I forget that some-times; so much of my life was get up, eat, go to school, go to SAT youth league meetings, eat, homework, sleep. But I finished, the one lone crèche student who made it through, all those youth group projects and sessions I led about what could be done to help keep everyone safe paying off. Bring-ing me here, to a job. To being a listener. It's an important job. Almost everyone keeps an eye on everyone they know for SAT, but being a listener is good. Much better than open-ing mail and then closing it up or spending days walking around stores trying to hear what other people say.

I look at the report. 56-412 was last reading and now—oh no. Over an hour has passed.

I did fall asleep. I check the receiver. It's still on.

It's still on, it's still recording, the sounds from 56-412's apartment being sent to the local security station and if he went out while I was asleep, if I missed something like that, I'll be sent back to the crèche and I swore I wouldn't go back, not ever, the only promise I've ever let myself believe, I was done with school I was working I was going to get an apartment, just a tiny one, and maybe, if I was lucky, get put on the list for a car, and now—

Now the attic door opens and I freeze, terrified security will have come, that something will have happened and that I've lost it all, this job, the life I've made. Any duties. All rights.

"Hi," someone says, but it isn't Security. They don't greet you, they take you away with the crook of a finger.

"I found a wire in the kitchen wall," the voice continues, and I turn, shocked because I know this voice, I've heard it once, twice, a dozen times or more now, muttering to himself while he reads. "So I thought I'd just come up and tell you what I'm doing *today. Save you the trouble of trying to figure it out from the sounds of me putting on my shoes and things."*

It is 56-412. He is here, right here, and he is looking at me.

He is looking at me and I feel the strangest, sharpest kick inside me, a race of fire rolling up my spine and clench-clutching my heart.

I look at him and I feel like I know him. Like I truly know him, like I have always known him.

But I've never seen him before.

18.

"YOU SHOULDN'T BE HERE," I say, and the teacher sighs.

"I think that's supposed to be my line," she says, and then gives me a little smile. "I could lecture you about sleeping in class but lunch is about to start and I'm sure you don't want to miss it."

"Lunch?" I say, confused because I was just awake and scared, worried because I wasn't hearing anything and then—

And then—

I don't know.

56-412 swims lazily through my mind, and I start to think of something, remember something—know something—and then my head begins to throb, tight pulsing pain.

"Yes, you have a split fourth period," she says. "Class, then lunch, then back here again. You really— you don't remember anything, do you?" She puts one hand on my desk. "I'm so sorry, Ava. Would you like me to walk you to the counselor?"

I know what a counselor is.

They look at files and then talk to you, soothing questions that build into something you can't get away from, and I can't see one, I can't, it'll be like being in that room again, back not knowing where 56-412 is, not knowing where he's gone.

He. It was a guy—56-412 was—is—a guy—and I saw him but I can't remember his face, try to picture it and get a stabbing pain in my head for my troubles, a bolt that lances from behind my eyes and down to my jaw.

"Are you sure?"

I nod and head into the hallway, moving as fast as my pain-filled head will allow. The teacher doesn't follow and I lean against the first solid surface I come to, closing my eyes against the pressure in my head. Against what I saw but can't quite remember.

Maybe it was a dream.

The pressure in my head eases then.

"Ava, there you are," a girl's voice says, and I open my eyes, see Olivia looking at me, anxiety making her flush hectic red along her forehead and cheeks. "Greer's waiting. Come on!"

I follow her, focusing on her, on everything I see, on

keeping my mind still so the pain will keep fading, will turn into a dull ache. We walk into a huge, open room filled with tables. One area, on the far right, holds students waiting with trays of food, popping in and out of lines, colorful cartons and bottles and boxes on display, waiting to be taken.

"You'd think they could serve us real food," Greer says as Olivia leads me over to a table. She pokes at a red box filled with french fries. "I mean, for the money we pay, they could hire at least one cook. One real cook. Sophy, please tell me you are not going to eat that."

"No, it was just there and I was in a hurry," Sophy says, and pushes away a sandwich, meat and bread and cheese wrapped in foil. The foil bumps into my hand as Olivia and I sit down. It's still warm.

Greer picks it up and tosses it in a nearby trash can, then starts picking at her fries. "Where were you during third?" she says.

It takes me a second to realize she's talking to me, because she's still looking at Sophy, as if she's waiting for something.

Sophy doesn't do anything though, just looks down at the table as if she's never seen anything like it before.

"Third?" I say, and then remember her asking me about it before. "I forgot."

"Forgot?" Greer says, and shakes her head. "I mean, I know you're no memory girl but, Ava, come on. Ethan was there. And he even asked about you."

"Ethan?" I say, thinking of the name in Ava's notebooks, written over and over again like it means something, everything, and Greer grins.

"I knew he'd be the one thing you wouldn't forget." She grins at Olivia, who opens a little brown paper bag and takes out a sandwich almost like Sophy's, only neatly wrapped in plastic. I wait for Greer to bat it away too, but she doesn't, just says, "Olivia, take these fries. I think Brandon is looking at me and I don't want him to think I'm a pig."

"Please, you're gorgeous," Olivia says, and grabs a few fries, turning the container toward me and Sophy. "You guys want some?"

I take a handful. Sophy shakes her head, finally looking up from the table to give Olivia a blindingly bright smile. "So, Brandon? What happened to Chuck? It's almost like no guy is good enough for you."

"Whatever. Chuck was boring," Greer says, looking

off into the distance, at someone behind me. "Brandon's way better-looking, too."

Olivia picks at the crust of her sandwich, shredding bits of it off.

"Right, Olivia?" Greer says, glancing back at us, at her, and Olivia smiles and nods.

"He *is* gorgeous, Greer," Sophy says, her voice animated, happy, and when I glance at her, wondering why she isn't eating the fries when she clearly wanted the sandwich, I see her looking at Olivia, a knowing smile curling her mouth.

What am I not seeing? I know it's something.

Olivia blinks, and then takes a bite of her sandwich.

"Soooooooooooooo," Greer says, looking at me again. "Don't you want to know what Ethan said?"

I'd rather know who he is, and what exactly is going on with Ava's so-called friends, but I settle for smiling and nodding. It seems to be what you do around Greer.

Greer tilts her head to one side, and gives me a long, measuring look. It doesn't have the power of Sophy's, but there's a depth to it, a strange sort of understanding. Of actual feeling.

"You don't remember him at all, do you?" she says, grinning, and then gets up. "Come with me."

I do, and she takes me out of the cafeteria, saying, "Female emergency!" to the male teacher sitting by the door, who frowns but sighs and motions for us to walk through an open door.

She leads me down one hall, and then another. "So you really don't remember anything? For real, I mean?"

I shake my head, and she stops. "What's it like? I mean, what do you see when you see me?"

I think: Someone who is very, very lucky. Someone who should watch out for Sophy because she's all quiet but gets grudgey, and clearly, usually against you.

But I just say, "I see someone who knows what ditching third is."

She stares at me, and then grins. "You don't even know what that is? For real?" She shakes her head. "Okay. During third period—which is study hall—we all meet outside in the back garden and hang out. You and me and Sophy and Olivia. We've been doing it since forever. But this year, you've been all distracted by—" She grabs my hand, and leads me down the hall a little more, stopping in front of a window.

"This," she says. "Look at the back row."

I look through the window. I see a classroom. In

the back row are four girls and three boys, each sitting at a desk. All of them are drawing, making long strokes with short gray sticks across huge sheets of white paper.

"You see him?" Greer says, and I know she means Ethan, the name Ava knows, the guy she knows, and start to shake my head, to lie and say "Yes," until I can figure it out, but then stop, all sound, all movement strangled inside me as one of the guys looks up.

Looks right at me.

I know him. Somehow, I know him. This Ethan.

But not the Ethan I see. I—

I know another one. The same, but different.

Like me, here. I look like the Ava I'm supposed to be.

But I'm not.

19.

GREER TAKES ME BACK to the cafeteria, laughing. "See? Part of you clearly remembers something
because the look on your face—" She sits down at the
table we've come back to. "Just like when you saw him
on the first day of school!"

I don't know what happened when I saw Ethan,
except that everything inside me just . . . froze. For
a second it felt like terror, like an icy hand grabbing
my heart, but then he smiled and I saw his hair, black
and curling down past his ears, and his eyes, wide and
warm and his smile, which was shy and happy and
knowing—and I smiled back. That made Greer grin
too, made her grin huge before she dragged me away.

"That was the best!" Olivia says, grinning at me.
"He came out into the garden and you just sort of—"
She makes her eyes go wide, drops her mouth open.
"Just like that, right, Greer?"

"Exactly like that. Hey, where are my fries?"

"Olivia finished them," Sophy says, and Greer sighs,
then rolls her eyes and says, "Whatever, I'll get some-

thing later. Okay, now, Ava, tell me everything you remember about Ethan. I mean, you don't remember us, but you remember him? What's up with that brain of yours, forgetting your best friends?"

"Yeah," Sophy says, echoing Greer, and I glance at her. See the sandwich she's nibbling on. See how she's smiling. Look back over at Olivia, who isn't eating anything anymore.

Sophy started with small stuff. Petty cruelty, barbs that stung. Then it was things she said during SAT youth meetings. Worries, she'd say. And smile.

And then bad things happened.

Sophy is—I don't know. Scary in what I know, but muted here.

Greer sees me looking and frowns. "Sophy, you said you were on a diet! You need more willpower, okay?" She takes the sandwich away from her and hands it back to Olivia, then looks at me, waiting.

Next to me, Sophy stiffens, but doesn't say a word.

"Have you—have you been in trouble lately?" I say to Sophy, who turns and looks at me as if I'm stupid.

"What does that mean?"

"I just—I thought maybe you might have done something or . . ."

Greer laughs. "Sophy do something wrong? Or worth noticing for more than a few seconds? Please!" She turns to Olivia and says, "Eat the sandwich, will you?"

"No, it's okay, I'm not hungry, really," Olivia says, but when she tries to pass the sandwich back to Sophy, Greer looks at her and says, "Olivia, I heard your stomach all through class," tossing an arm around her and pulling her close for a second.

Olivia's eyes flutter closed, then open as Greer moves away. I see the look in Olivia's eyes though, and when I glance at Sophy and then Greer, I see Sophy sees it too. Sees who Olivia longs for. She carries her heart in her eyes.

"Well, Ava, talk," Greer says, and next to me, Sophy grins a small, almost hidden smile.

"I don't remember him," I say.

"Hi, I saw you when you saw him, and you definitely knew something," Greer says.

"It was—I don't know how to say it," I say, even though I really do.

"You thought he was cute," Olivia says, her voice understanding, and when I glance at her she looks at Greer. "You can totally tell from her face. But you don't really remember him, do you? It's more like—it's more like you remember the idea of him. The cute guy, the awesome friends. Right?" She smiles.

I smile back at her, because even though she isn't exactly right, she's trying, and her smile is real, without the tension and show of Greer's. Without the banked anger and longing-for-be power of Sophy's.

"Oh," Greer says, looking disappointed, and then she grins. "Well, we'll just have to tell you everything about Ethan. And you and Ethan. Sophy, will you get me some more fries?" She looks at me. "Do you remember how Sophy was a complete and utter grade-obsessed loser with no friends before we started hanging out with her?"

Sophy gets up and stalks away.

"Greer," Olivia says, and Greer shakes her head.

"She took your sandwich, Olivia. Someone has to stand up for you, and until you get a decent guy, it'll have to be me."

Olivia turns back to me. "Now, Ethan."

It turns out there isn't much to know about Ava and Ethan. Ava has liked him since the beginning of the school year, when he transferred in, and so far they've talked twice. Once he asked her what time it was, and once, when they were all sitting outside, she asked him how he was. He said, "Fine." This, apparently, happened right before Ava lost her memory.

Right before me.

There's a little bit more to know about Ethan. He's new. ("Obviously," as Greer tells me, and then, "Well, except that you forgot. Sorry.") His mother is supposedly recently married to a really rich guy and they all live in an amazing—and expensive—house that Olivia's mother swears is made of almost all glass and is actually built so it looks like it's part of a nearby forest.

"It's up on stilts or beams or something, and it's like it's in the trees, you know?" Olivia says. "His stepdad or whatever he calls him is really strict, though. Ethan has like, a fifth-grade curfew. It's insane."

"I heard nobody's even seen his house, so the whole forest house thing might not be true," Sophy says, sitting back down, and Olivia blushes.

"Just because you haven't seen it doesn't mean anything," Greer says. "Olivia's mom works with a guy whose wife sold the house, so you know she's seen it. Why are you being all weird today?"

"I—I'm not," Sophy says. Softly, but with so much steel behind it. "And you and Olivia haven't seen his

ELIZABETH SCOTT

house. No one has. Ethan doesn't even ever talk about
it. It's like he doesn't have a home. Maybe he just says
he does."

"Except he *does*, and you know it," Greer says, wav-
ing one hand at her. "Clearly, the best chance anyone
has to see this forest house is sitting right here." She
grins at me. "Because now we get to the most important part, the one where he asked about you."

"It's true, he did," Olivia says. "He said, 'How's
Ava?' So see, he totally knows your name!"

And then she and Greer look at me, waiting.

"Oh," I say.

Greer laughs, and after a second, Olivia does too,
Sophy joining in as well.

"If you could remember," Greer says, still laughing,
"you'd be saying so much more than 'oh' right now.
But hey, now you're all mysterious because you don't
remember anything and you are so going to get him. I
mean, you're the only girl he's ever asked about, as far
as I know. He's not much of a talker. So show up at the
garden tomorrow, okay?"

"During third," Olivia adds and I nod.

The bell rings then, and everyone gets up and hugs
and waves and then disappears, although Sophy shoots

me a glance after she hugs me, like she's looking for something in my eyes.

I start to call out after her as she walks away and then stop, remembering the smile on her face when she saw Olivia's heart in her eyes. Sophy is someone to watch.

I know how to do that, don't I?

I shiver—*memory, Morgan, cold*—and make myself think about Ethan as I head back to class. There was— is—something about him. Something I can't quite see, a . . . a memory just out of reach. But it's there, and knowing that is the most I've had since I woke up.

I spend the rest of the day looking at his name in Ava's notebook and wondering if I'll see him again.

I don't.

20.

JANE PICKS ME UP AFTER SCHOOL, and I
have to think of something to call her, I am avoiding
"Mom" and she knows it, I see her face when she says,
"Ava, honey, hi!" and I say, "Hi," and nothing more in
return.

It's one word but I can't say it, I don't feel it, she
doesn't feel like "Mom" to me, I don't look at her and
think "family," but it's hurting her and that makes me
feel bad, not like the weird, quick lurch of sensation
that hit me when I first saw Ethan, but something bigger, deeper.

It's not her fault I don't know her.

We're going to see one of my doctors, a neurologist
I only saw once in the hospital and don't remember
because it happened back when they were keeping me
sedated so I wouldn't ask them where I was and who
I was over and over again, when they were trying to
keep me "calm."

When we get out of the car at the doctor's office
and head in, she walks a little ahead of me, saying,

"You don't need to be nervous, okay?" her own voice shaking, and her hair streams back behind her in the wind.

I reach up and touch a strand as it blows near my face and suddenly my hand is my hand—a hand I know, a hand I remember, smaller and thinner, younger, but my hand.

My hand, touching Jane's hair. It happened. I know it. I see it.

I remember it.

"I—" I say, stopping, and when she turns to face me I see her now but through that, around it, I see her again, looking younger but older, dark circles under her eyes, the bones of her face pushing against her skin, which is colored gray-white, as if she's becoming a shadow.

It's Jane, but not this Jane, not the one from this place. This Ava's life.

It's a different Jane. A Jane I know.

I see her, though, *remember* her, and in my memory Jane smiles at me, a sad smile, and there is darkness around her, it hurts my head when I try to see through it, but when she lifts one hand I say, *"Mom?"*

I say it, call out "Mom?" but she doesn't turn around,

*she is leaving, turning away, I can see her feet moving, al-
most like she is floating, as if she is being carried off and—*

"Ava?" Jane says, and she is staring at me, her face
full and bright with color, red hope blooming across
her cheeks. "What did you just say?"

"I saw you," I say. "I—just now. I saw you. I remembered you. You looked younger but sad and something—someone was taking you—" Something in my
head pops, a weird sparking sensation at the back of
my skull that clamps pain down around my head, cir-
cling from front to back, so sudden and strong that my
breath hitches out of me, my whole body sagging like
it wants to fall through the ground.

"Ava, honey, it's all right," Jane says, pulling me up
and close, sheltering me against her.

"My head," I say and she rubs my back, says, "I
know, I know," telling me to keep my eyes closed,
steering me into the building like I'm blind, whispering, "You called me Mom," into my hair over and over
again.

The pain in my head eases while we wait for the
doctor, only coming back when I try to picture the
Jane I saw—the other one, the younger and sadder

one—and what was around her when she left, what took her away.

Dr. Jabar, the neurologist, is pleased by what's happened, and makes me tell him everything even though Jane is practically vibrating with joy and the need to talk about it. I do, even though it makes my head hurt again, and at the end I look at Jane and realize I still can't call her Mom in my head even though I remembered her.

I don't know why I can't say that word.

"Ava's case is most interesting," Dr. Jabar tells Jane. "This memory, today, is a good sign. You know, the only thing remotely unusual about any of the scans we did is that we found evidence that Ava had a mild case of rickets as a child. That's unusual these days, but no cause for amnesia."

"Rickets?" Jane says. "What's that?"

"Lack of vitamin D," Dr. Jabar says. "It used to be more common before the vitamin was added to milk. Did Ava not like milk as a child?"

Jane nods, looking anxious, and Dr. Jabar says, "That's not so unusual. My own daughter refuses to drink milk or eat meat of any kind." He shrugs. "But usually sunlight provides enough vitamin D, so, I'm wondering, was Ava very sick as a child for an extended period of time, perhaps? An illness that required her to stay indoors?"

The walls around us, neutral-colored, soothing, turn gray, and the windows that let in the sun go dark, framed with wire.

I am so tired of the dark and the gray and the walls that never ever end. And I am cold, so cold. I look around, desperate, alone, always alone and knowing I have to get out, that I can't be here, I won't be here, not now, not ever, I have to get out, I will get out, I will. I have—there is something I have to do. Like there is something—someone I have to find. It gives me—in the dark and cold night, when I'm shivering, I tell myself I have to leave. Not just because I want to, but because I have to.

Because I will.

"Ava?" Jane says, touching my hand and I shake my head, pain sloshing around inside it, pushing back and forth from my eyes to the base of my skull. But the walls aren't gray anymore and I'm not alone. I can feel Jane's hand against mine.

"Are you all right?" Dr. Jabar says, and when I nod,

says, "Good, good," and then launches into a discussion about my brain.

"Can I get some water?" I ask Jane, because my head hurts and I don't care about my brain, not when it hurts like this, and Jane nods and smiles at me.

I get up and walk out, heading through the main part of the office, where all the patients wait.

In the hallway, I wander around, half looking for a water fountain, half just not wanting to go back and look at him. Dr. Jabar's office is in a building full of them, the hallway covered with doors that look the same except for the names printed on them. I bet all four floors are just like this one.

I find a water fountain hidden in a corner. It doesn't work, only hisses when I press for water. The ladies room is right next to it, just behind me.

In the bathroom, I wash my hands, then cup water into them and drink. When I look at my face in the mirror, I don't recognize it, it is alien but familiar in a way that twists my stomach. I turn away quickly, heading for the door.

As I leave, someone comes in, moving fast and bumping into me, and then I'm back in the bathroom, staring at a guy who is standing pressed against the door. Standing staring at me.

He is my age, and thin, with desperate brown eyes, and when he talks his voice is so thick with fear I can almost taste it. "Ava, are you okay? Tell me you're okay. I didn't know this would happen, I swear and now—"

He crosses to me, moving closer, and I can only stare, trapped by the fear and longing I see in his eyes, but the knowledge there, the knowledge of me and a million other things.

He knows me. The Ava I am.

He *knows* me.

And I—I *know* him.

I know him from the attic, but in a blinding, crippling flash I see him looking at me in a desert, I see me looking at him in a hallway, I see us looking at each other, both dressed in long robes while fans flutter around us.

I have always known him, and I stare, waiting.

"I found you," he says, his voice easing, and reaches a hand out toward my face, to touch me, and I, despite what I just saw, what I *know*—I take a step back.

He stops then, surprise on his face, and says, "I'm so sorry, I know you must be angry but please, I didn't know this was going to happen, that she would do this. You have to know that. You have to . . ." He trails off, looking into my eyes like he should see something there, and then he is shaking his head, leaning forward and saying, "No, no, no," in a broken whisper, pressing his hands against his legs.

He looks at me then, pleading on his face, on the curve of his lips, and I turn away, racing for the door. The mention of *she* has made me feel bad, so, so bad.

Like I'm dying bad.

Like I-know-something-that-I-can't-see-bad. I clutch my stomach.

When I reach the door, he says, "It's me, Morgan," his voice whisper-soft, like a prayer, and behind the pain in my head something sparks open, shaking free.

Morgan. MORGAN, 56-412, and I know that, I know those numbers, I know the word. The name. The place. We have always known each other but now I see the attic.

"I—" I say and then I am there.

I'm in the attic, pulling my headset off as I turned to see the voice I know but the face I should never see, the face that should never see me, and there he is, 56-412 looking right at me, brown eyes, short brown hair, my age and as surprised as I am, I see it in his eyes, he has eyes you can see everything in, and I say, "Morgan," my voice as quiet as the ghost I am supposed to be.

"Ava," Morgan says, and I am back in the bathroom now, mirror in front of me, reflecting sinks and toilet stalls and shimmering within them a tiny wooden room with an orange chair waiting. Two rooms, two places, except I have a feeling that if I looked closer I would see more rooms, more places, more of me and him.

Of us.

I blink, scared but not, awake like I haven't felt since I first woke up in Ava's house, in Ava's bed, and look at him.

"I didn't think it would be so hard to find you," he says. "I didn't even think I'd make it here. There isn't a me here so I'm not supposed to be here. Also, everything is very strange, not at all like home and—" He blows out a breath, looking off to the side and then back at me as if he's afraid I will vanish. There are freckles on his face, a tiny patch on his nose, and there are shadows under his eyes, deep and dark. A cut on his neck. Shadows of bruises on his jaw, faded faint yellow-green. I want to touch them, smooth them away.

I want to touch him.

He's looking at me as if the whole world waits for my next breath, with an intensity that makes my heart pound and my palms sweat and then he smiles, a sweet curve of his mouth, and my breath catches, but then I freeze because there is something about it, something beyond it that I know, that makes my mind go blank with fear and pain. I shrink back and the room is a dream, the orange chair is a dream, I remembered Jane, I was here, I am here.

I look at him, and then I close my eyes. Maybe I'm crazy.

Maybe I'm scared.

"Ava," he whispers, pleading, but I keep them closed. I have to find out what is real. I have to wake up for real.

"Hey," someone says, and I open my eyes slowly, knowing Morgan will be gone. It is not his voice I just heard.

But he isn't gone, he is still here, still looking at me. He is here and the only change is that now a security guard is too, peering at my face and pulling Morgan's arms tight behind him, so he can't touch me. Can't reach me.

I don't like that.

"Are you all right?" the security guard asks and I stare at him blankly because I thought I was dreaming when I closed my eyes and fell into the attic, into listening, into hearing that voice. Hearing Morgan.

I stare and Morgan says, "I'm sorry, Ava, I'm so sorry, maybe if there was a place here for me things would be better, maybe you and me—" and then jerks his arms free, the security guard stumbling back, saying, "Hey!" and grabbing at empty space as Morgan pulls the bathroom door open and runs through it.

The guard runs out into the hall, leaving me standing there in the bathroom. In the mirror I see my face, my open eyes.

I close them. After a moment, the door opens again.

"Ava?" Jane says. "Oh, Ava," and her voice is shaking and she is shaking, and the security guard is saying, "I'm so glad that woman called and said she thought she saw something, I'm so glad I got here—wait, hold on. Jerry, what do you mean you don't see him? He ran down the stairs, how could you not see him?"

"You're all right?" Jane says, touching my arms, my face, my shoulders, and I draw back, nodding, thinking of him looking at me. Of me looking back.

Of how I remember something other than that brief, strange glimpse of a faraway, different Jane and me.

I remember him.

I remember Morgan in a way I didn't—can all that I saw be memories?

I know at least one of them is for sure.

I know that I am from a place that is like this one but different, so different.

But how did I end up here?

And what did Morgan mean when he said there wasn't a him here? How can that matter?

I don't know. I just know that Morgan—that I know him.

I know him better than anyone here.

21.

JANE FOLLOWS ME around when we get back to the house, asking if I need anything. Something to drink? To eat?

"I'm fine," I say, sitting on her sofa and trying to think—to remember—even though it makes my head pound so hard spots of yellow and red dance in front of my eyes.

I'm not from here. That's the drumbeat of words in my head, pounding along to the pain in my skull.

I don't belong here. I'm not the Ava who's supposed to be here.

I'm from somewhere else.

Somewhere that isn't here.

"I have to check my work voice mail, but I'll be right in the kitchen," Jane says. "Call me if you need anything." And then she stands there, hovering, waiting.

Looking worried.

"I really am fine," I tell her, the words coming out

poorly, shaking, and she looks like she wants to cry and hug me. In the end, she settles for squeezing one of my hands, gently, and saying, "Anything, okay?"

Anything. Tell me why I'm here. Tell me where I came from. Tell me why I remembered you, but a different you.

Tell me who I am.

I get up, head for the front door. Jane comes out from the kitchen, hand over the phone. "Ava?"

"I need to—I want to go out," I say.

"Out?" Jane says, worry in her voice. "But what if the boy from before . . . ? You have to stay on the porch, all right, Ava? And you should leave the front door open too. You have to stay safe."

I nod and walk outside. Jane sounds so scared.

I look back in the open door. Jane is peering into the hallway, glancing at me as she talks on the phone.

She hadn't said anything as the security guard walked us out of the bathroom, and when he asked her, gently, if she knew "the young man," she shook her head, looked bewildered and terrified.

"Why did he come here?" she'd said. "What did he—why did he come after Ava?"

When she said that, I wondered what had happened to her Ava. Why she—I—whoever I was—woke up knowing nothing.

What if it wasn't an infection no one had noticed?

What if it was something else?

Jane had asked me if I knew him—Morgan—on the way home, her hands holding the steering wheel so tight they were stone-white, bloodless looking.

"I—I've never seen him here," I said, because I hadn't—not here, not in this place—and I didn't think what was in my strange, empty but not empty head would count.

But it did. It does.

"I was so scared," Jane said. "I can't bear another—I don't want anything to happen to you."

Now I look at her, watching me, and wave, to show I am all right. That I am here. She relaxes, a little, and after a few minutes, turns away frowning and holding the phone like she can only hear it twisted a certain way, walking back into the kitchen as she does.

I look around. The lawn; the grass I stood on that first night, it still looks the same. The street still looks the same. It looks like the moment when I realized I didn't know where I was. That I don't know who I am.

My skin goes cold suddenly, goose pimples rolling up my arms, and I watch a car turn into the driveway, rolling to a stop just out of sight of the front door. Just out of sight of Jane.

I start to turn to call her, but then the car door opens and Clementine gets out. My heart starts to beat fast, skipping and stuttering in my chest, and when I try to look away from her, I can't.

When she smiles at me, the goose bumps grow sharper, and a chill races up my spine.

"Stopped by to give you this," she says, and hands me a box with a pie in it.

I turn away and she leans over, places it next to me on the steps. She smells strange. Cold. I didn't know cold had a smell but it does, a bitter chill that makes my insides sting.

"You look tired," she says. "Has anything . . . stressful happened to you today?" There is a note of something in her voice, under the sugar-sweet softness of her tone.

She sounds . . . worried.

I look at her now, watching her face. "Like remembering who I am?"

"Well, that's a given. You're supposed to do that,

right?" Clementine says with a smile that pulls at something inside of me. That reminds me of something. Someone—

I don't know.

I can't remember, and my head is starting to ache again.

"Why are you making my head hurt?"

Clementine blinks at me, looking surprised, but then says, "Headaches are normal for people who've—"

"It only happens when I think about certain things. People."

"That shouldn't be happening," she mutters, but before I can ask her what she means, Jane says, "Clementine?" coming to the door. "I thought I heard a car. What are you doing here?"

"I just stopped by to see how Ava is," Clementine says, picking up the pie and giving it to Jane.

"You shouldn't have done this," Jane says, and she sounds very nice. Very polite.

She also sounds like she means what she said, that she doesn't want Clementine to have come here.

I look at her and see that she doesn't like Clementine. I watch how her eyes move, how she blinks.

I see she is afraid.

Why?

"Oh, it was nothing," Clementine says. "I just—well, you know how talk gets around the hospital and one of the nurses at Dr. Jabar's called over to get some records sent and said that there was some sort of problem with Ava today."

"Not with Ava," Jane says. "Ava's fine."

"But I heard that—"

"My head hurts," I say to Jane, cutting Clementine off. "Can we go in?"

"Oh, honey, of course," Jane says, relief in her voice, and holds the door open for me as we walk inside. I look back before it closes and see Clementine still standing there watching us. Watching me.

She came here because of what happened at Dr. Jabar's today.

Because of Morgan. I know it. I *know it*.

She wanted to see if I'd seen him.

I think she wants to know if I remember him.

Why?

22.

THAT NIGHT I sit on the floor of Ava's room, going over the furniture with my fingertips in the dark, waiting to remember it. It's starting to feel familiar, but that isn't memory.

My mind has nothing but blankness behind a few bits and pieces of things that don't add up. I remember Jane, but a different Jane, a Jane that left me, was taken away.

And Morgan. I remember him, this afternoon. The dreams I've had, the attic and the cold and him.

They aren't dreams. I want to think they are, I want to think they have to be—this doesn't happen to people, they don't wake up and find themselves somewhere else but they aren't dreams.

They're memories.

They're memories and if Morgan is real, and here, then how can I remember him—and me—somewhere else? Not to mention how I saw us in all those other times so fast, like there has always been him and me.

Like we have always found each other.

I don't know how.

I just know what I saw. What I felt.

I walk out into the hallway. I know its darkness now too, and head for one of the closed doors, let myself into Ava's bathroom.

I like Ava's bathroom best out of every room in the house. I like her large white shower, her broad sink. I like the bottles and jars of lotion she has, like opening them up and sniffing them even though I can't bring myself to use them, find myself clutching the large bar of soap she has in her shower each time I use it as if I have never seen it before.

I haven't, not that I remember, but shouldn't I be used to soap? Shouldn't I not be so amazed by how it is so large and all mine?

I fall asleep in there, holding one of Ava's soft, thick towels and a jar of mango-ginger body lotion, and wake up to see Jane looking at me, her face lit by the hall light and the sun that cuts through it from the open door of Jane's bedroom.

"Did you sleep in here?" she says.

"I—" I say, and sit up, my body stiff from being

curled up on the floor. Somehow, it feels more familiar than waking up in the softness of Ava's bed. "I guess I did."

Jane sits down next to me, touching the bottle of lotion.

"I keep telling Ava not to waste her money on things like that, but she . . ." She trails off.

"But she what?"

"But you keep buying it," she says, smiling at me, but too late, too late, we both know what she said.

Ava. Her. She.

Not you.

Not one You.

I look at Jane. "I—I'm not her, am I? I'm not Ava."

Jane stares at me.

"Don't," she finally says, looking at the floor, and then says it again, louder, before looking at me.

There are tears in her eyes.

My heart pounds.

"Don't ever—please don't ever think that," she says. "I can't—just hearing you say it . . . You don't really think that, do you? I know it's hard for you and that things aren't the same. The doctors said . . . they said you might not ever remember everything. That things might be a little different. That you might be a little different. But you're still Ava. You'll always—you're forever my little girl."

"But just now you said—"

"I know," she says. "I'm—I'm tired, honey. I'm scared. I lie awake at night worrying about you. Wondering what it must be like to be here, with me, and to not know—" She breaks off. "Sometimes I think you must be so angry with me."

"Angry?"

"You're so—Ava, you're so quiet now, and I—" She takes a deep breath. "I can't believe I'm saying this, but I miss you yelling at me. You used to, you know, all the time, over your clothes, your hair, everything. But now you—you're so nice to me. And I love it but I look at you and I know you don't—you don't remember me."

"I did—"

"I know," she says. "But one time, honey, and I—it's something I don't actually remember. I've been thinking about it all night and I just . . . it's not there. I can't see it." She touches my hair with one hand, gently. "Is that what it's like for you? Is that how—is that how everything is, you try to remember but nothing's there?"

"Yes," I say, my voice cracking, shocking me, making me cringe, and she says, "Oh, Ava," and folds her hands together like she doesn't know what to do with them. Like she doesn't know what to do about anything.

"I'm sorry," she says after a while. "I know that doesn't make things better, but I wish it did. I wish I could. I wanted—I want you here and happy and safe."

"I want—" I say, and then have to stop because I don't know what words should come after those. I don't know what I want.

And then Jane looks at me, so much sadness and worry—so much love—in her eyes—and I wish I could help her. I wish I could make things better for her. Be the Ava I'm supposed to be.

But I can't.

I'm not her.

It's a relief to get to school, or at least it is until third period, when I leave study hall like Greer and Olivia and Sophy told me to and make my way to the garden.

"There you are," Greer says when she sees me. "What happened to you this morning, you wench? We totally waited for you."

"Late," I say, thinking of the silent, strained breakfast Jane and I had shared, and the equally silent ride to school.

How Jane had leaned toward me when we stopped, like she wanted to hug me and then stilled, able to tell I didn't know what to do. That my arms weren't opening for her.

The look on her face when I got out of the car . . .

It made me think of the Jane I know, that I remember.

It made me want to open my arms but it was too late, I was out of the car and at school, swimming around in Ava's life.

"Well, stop it," Greer says. "Here's a memory I'll fill in for you: I don't wait. Ever. Okay?"

"Greer," Olivia says, elbowing her, and Greer rolls her eyes and says, "I'm kidding, Ava," and looks at Olivia. "Thanks, Mom."

Olivia giggles, and then turns away when she sees me looking at her.

She knows I see what's in her heart. Who's in it, and it makes her face turn deep, dark red.

How can Greer not see this?

"Guys, shut up," Greer says. "Ava, don't look, but you-know-who is coming this way."

"I know who," Sophy says, her voice a singsong

mockery of Greer's, and Greer and Olivia both look at her, Greer with both eyebrows raised, Olivia merely looking startled.

"We all know who, duh," Greer says, rolling her eyes at Sophy, and then grins at me. "Well, don't just stand there. Sit down and smile. But not at him! Smile at Sophy and then laugh like she's said something funny. You'll have to pretend hard for that one."

Sophy, who is sitting down on a bench next to me, looks up at me, smiles, and pats the space next to her. The tips of her ears are a mottled, angry red.

I sit down, forcing my mouth into a smile, and look at the cover of the textbook Sophy's fiddling with. The top right corner looks like it's been gouged with something sharp, but the rest of the cover is spotless, the map that covers it glowing brown and green and blue, the whole world sketched out and divided up along curving lines.

It seems to grow larger, and paler, faded with age, and I shake my head to clear it, closing my eyes.

"Hey," I hear, and open my eyes, see Ethan sitting next to me. His hair is short, cropped close to his scalp, raw red and freshly cut. He is taking furious, frantic notes.

"Hey," I say, and he looks at me, sort of, a sideways, almost anxious glance.

"What are you doing here?" I say.

"You're making fun of me too?" he says, his voice low and miserable. "I passed the first maps class, Ava. I did, I swear. And besides, you—you shouldn't even be talking to me. You're crèche, and just because Greer talks to you it doesn't mean the rest of us can. You know how—you know how things are." He turns away and opens a small tin on his desk, takes out a peppermint.

"Sorry," he mutters after a moment. "I didn't mean it. I'm just . . . you know how bad I am with maps. I didn't really—I—" His voice cracks, and then he crunches the mint between his teeth and starts taking notes again.

"Is this a memory?" I say, but he's silent, his mouth not moving even though he says "Ava."

I hear it though, hear him, and I lean toward him, everything going blurry, fading as a headache bursts open behind my eyes, blinding me.

"Ava, sit up!" I hear, and blink, see Sophy next to me, watching me. See Olivia smiling at me, hear Greer saying, "Ava, sit up!" again.

"Oh," I say, sliding back onto the bench, my head

throbbing, and Ethan is standing a few feet away, looking at me.

He doesn't look the same. His hair isn't short, it's
longish like it was before, when Greer took me to see
him, and has fallen so it shadows the side of his face,
dark curls ringing the slight fullness of his cheeks,
stopping by the curve of his lips. He has a full, smiling
mouth.

He doesn't look miserable. He looks happy.

I don't understand.

But then I know I remember Ethan, but not this
Ethan.

But why is this Ethan so happy when the Ethan I
know wasn't?

What am I not seeing?

As he sees me watching him, he winks and gives
me a slow, small wave, a suggestive crooking of his
fingers. When I don't wave back, he gives a little sigh
and then another, slightly smaller smile, like a secret,
before he turns and walks away.

He looks so happy. So calm.

But his smile never touched his eyes, not even a
little.

His eyes are . . .

They're sad. They're full of knowing that no one should have.

I know this Ethan's eyes.

"Gah!" Greer says, grabbing my arm as the bell rings. "That was a total I-want-you thing, there. I wanted to have sex just watching you two."

"I know," Olivia says. "Ava, you should go for it already, okay? I mean, we all know what you're thinking when you look at him, and now he's totally thinking it too."

He was? I didn't see it. I didn't—I didn't feel anything. Not then. The maps—then I felt something.

I felt sorry for him.

"Are you all right?" Sophy says, touching my arm as Greer and Olivia head off to their classes. "I know you don't actually remember Ethan—or anyone—and, well—we used to talk a lot about stuff, you know?"

I look at her, and I can't tell if she's lying or not. I can't read her.

It makes me nervous.

"I'm okay," I say, and when she smiles I see another smile under the one she wears, a deeper one, a stronger one. One that has power and uses it. Loves it.

Destroys with it, or wants to.

I know her too. Not this her, but another her, and that Sophy—

That Sophy was everything this one wants to be.

I shudder.

I'm Ava, I remember people from this place.

I remember them, but not from here.

How can I remember a world that isn't mine? One that isn't the one I wake up in every day now?

"Girls, get to class," a teacher passing by calls out, and I'm glad to turn away.

Glad to walk away.

23.

IN CHEMISTRY CLASS, I don't understand why the teacher is going over the periodic table so slowly, or why he isn't talking about the way each element can be used.

I don't know how I know the elements, or what they can do. Ava's notes for this class are as empty as all her others. I doodle a little, copying Ava's squares and spirals and then a few squiggles of my own, attaching letters and numbers to them that don't mean anything but flow out of my pen anyway and then sigh, pull out my English textbook and hide it inside my Chemistry book.

English, like Government, it's another class I am lost in, startled by references to things everyone seems to know about but that I can't remember. Today we talked about pastoral imagery, which seems to mean that sheep and grass are more than just sheep and grass.

I look at the poem again, and manage to get about twenty lines in before my eyes start to feel heavy. I

ELIZABETH SCOTT

like the idea of green grass, of open spaces. It sounds
so free.

*I wish I could see grass like that, green grass, I think, and
wake up with a start, jerking up so hard my chair squeaks.
I look around, but the attic is empty and I let out a sigh.*

*Relief, I tell myself, relief, and rub my eyes, tell myself to
stop dreaming and listen.*

Nothing.

*I adjust my headset, flex my fingers over the keyboard,
and then type "56-412 watches television and eats chips."*

*After that lie—another one, already—I look at my own
small foil packet. The bread is so heavy it's poked through
one corner, dense brown that can only be tamed through
thick mustard.*

I wonder where Morgan is. I wish—

*No. I have got to stop doing this, I can't drift away, I
have to stay here. I've worked so hard. It has been all I ever
wanted.*

Thought I wanted.

*"Ava," he says quietly—he's here, again—and I turn
around, the chair wheezing protest. It was not meant to
move so fast.*

*"You have to stop coming up here," I say, but I don't
mean it, watching as he pulls the attic door closed, and my*

*heart is pounding from him, just from him, and I know, I
know, I know him, it is the beating of my heart.*

*But what if someone saw him come up here? I am in the
attic and he is on the top floor, in his own apartment, an
unheard of luxury, but there are SAT everywhere.*

*I talk to the one low-level watcher who lives on the first
floor every week and she tells me what Morgan bought at
the grocery store because he always stops by to say "Hello"
since they have to wait in the same line together. She is sure
he always gets sausages when she never gets any. She thinks
he must know someone, or that he is a thief. She wants to
get proof so she can get him sent away and get an extra card
for rations every month.*

*Sometimes I think life outside the crèche is no better than
life in it.*

*"Why can't I come up here?" he says and comes closer,
moving so he is standing in front of me, then kneeling so I
can see into his eyes, he can see into mine, I try to turn away
but he puts his hands on my knees, not hard, not hard at all,
his touch is so gentle, his thumbs moving in a slow circle. I
feel myself sinking into the touch, into him.*

*Into us, and that's just it—I see him and I see me and
him and we—I close my eyes.*

"I have to listen to you," I say, trying to make my voice

strong, and when I open my eyes he smiles, a small, crooked smile, and says, "But I'm right here."

"I can't—" I say and my voice is cracking because I'm scared someone has seen us—him—that's all, I'm not scared of him, I'm not scared of what I think when I see him. What I feel.

Alive.

"I think about you listening to me," he says. "You hear everything, don't you?"

I bite my lip because I do, of course I do, and I know what his breathing in bed this morning meant, I wrote "56-412 masturbates," and then sat, fingers shaking before I gave in and touched myself, thinking of him and wondering—hoping—he was thinking of me.

"I can have you taken in," I say and he draws back a little. The sun, filtered in through the small, dirty windows, catches his eyes. They are brown, ordinary, but the way he looks at me—no one has ever looked at me like he does. He looks at me like he sees something. Someone.

Me.

"All right," he says, and puts his hands behind his head. "Go ahead."

24.

WAKE UP.

I don't want to, I want what's next, I want to be there, with him, and I—

"Wake up," I hear, and sit up, disoriented, my English book falling out of my Chemistry book and hitting the desk.

I was here. I was in class, I am in class. I wasn't in an attic, I didn't see Morgan. We didn't talk, we didn't do anything. But it—

It felt so real. Embarrassingly real.

Frighteningly real.

Alive real.

"What's this?" the chemistry teacher says, and he's the one who told me to wake up just now.

I heard it twice, though. He said it and then before . . . before it didn't sound like a voice at all. It was something else, it was action, I was being pulled back, away.

"I said, what's this?" the chemistry teacher says again, pointing not at my fallen English book, but at my notebook, at the little branching sticks with number and letters appended to them that I drew, a squiggle tagged $C_3H_6N_6O_6$.

"I don't know."

"You think you're funny?" he says, voice rising on every word. "We're studying chemistry here, and you—you think drawing the formula for a lethal explosive is a good idea?"

"I—"

"Go to the office right now!" he says, and strangely, his anger and the way everyone around me falls silent because it feels far more familiar than all the other classes I've sat through, like somehow I'm used to being silent in class.

To being scared.

In the office, I'm told to sit and wait, that Jane will be called.

"You know about Mr. Green's son and what he did, of course," the woman who calls Jane tells me when she gets off the phone.

When I stare at her blankly, she clears his throat and says, "I—Sorry, Ava. Why don't you spend the rest of the period in the nurse's office while we wait for your mother."

It's not a question.

I get up, but instead of going to the nurse's office I head outside, wanting to get away from the school and whatever is going on with me. This morning, with Ethan, and then just now, what happened, what I dreamed—

No. What I know.

What I remember.

Not that this Ethan is one I know, not that he's someone I remember. No one here—except for Morgan and Clementine—reaches into that strange, hazy place inside me. In my head.

But still, somehow, someway, I remember a different Ethan. A different Jane. It's like some people—Jane, Sophy, Olivia, Greer, Ethan—that are in this Ava's life were . . .

Were somehow, and in very different ways, in memories that I'm not supposed to have.

Were in a life I know better—deeper, truer—than this one.

When I get outside, I look for Jane's car even though I know it won't be here yet. It isn't. There is nothing to see but a guy sitting on the white stone bench by the street, watching me.

Morgan.

When he sees me looking, he stands up. Walks toward me, stepping carefully across the road. He doesn't look like he belongs here. There is something not quite right about him; the way he walks, as if every step pains him, and how he looks around, as if everything he sees is unknown, not terrifying but new.

"I know you," I say, and he smiles like I have given him the world.

"I would have come sooner," he says. "You know that, don't you? I just—it was hard to find you."

"Why?" I say, and his mouth opens, but no sound comes out. The world flutters, then drifts.

Shifts.

25.

WAKE UP.

I sit up, startled and blinking, and realize I've slid off the orange chair again. I know it's nothing but bad color and creaks and cracks, but to slide right off it?

I've got to stop falling asleep. I've got to stop sitting up at night staring at my hands and thinking about what I've typed. About Morgan.

I've got to stop wondering—wishing. I know what happens to people who do, poor Olivia with her heart in her eyes even as her brains were clubbed across the floor for not saying who she was sleeping with, Olivia dying as Greer stood next to me, shaking but watching without blinking.

You don't question what happens, not ever, and I don't want to die.

But he's here. I know it, can hear him before I see him, and when I turn around Morgan is in the attic again. Sitting right next to me. Looking at me.

I have to report this. Report him. I haven't done it yet, but I will, I will.

My fingers don't move. Don't type.

"*You must have fallen off the chair,*" *he says, and I see there is a shirt tucked under me, soft fabric wedged near the edge of my head, as if someone has tried to slip it under me.* "*Don't you ever sleep?*"

"*Yes, I sleep,*" *I say, and shove his shirt back at him, trying not to notice how soft the cloth is and failing. I have to stop this. I have to.*

Something is off with him. I can't afford clothes like his. Even if I do well, I could serve the government for ten, fifteen years—a lifetime—before I would even be let into the stores that sell shirts like his.

It takes a long time to move past being crèche. I was told that before I started training, reminded of it every day, in the years it took for me to make the few friends I have: Greer, Olivia, and Ethan. The three people who didn't mind talking to me even though they came from where I want to be and I'm from where no one wants to go.

"*You look tired,*" *Morgan says, as if we are talking, as if he wants to talk, and I stare at him because we—he—can't talk to me like this. I'm a listener now, I clawed my way out of a bed shared by four, in a hall shared by hundreds, to be someone. To be here. To listen to him, who has more than I can ever hope for and doesn't seem to care that he's so close to being lost. To disappearing.*

"Why are you here?" That is the one thing I can't work out. I know there are always some who must test the government, that they can't help themselves. But he does not organize protests in his apartment, doesn't have dinners with careful conversations that will have to be picked apart. He goes to school, he reads, he eats. He lives.

I don't know why he is being watched. But then, I am not supposed to know. He just is, like most everyone is at one time or another, and I am not even supposed to think about it. I am just supposed to listen. To be invisible to him, and report on what I hear.

I am not supposed to be sitting here watching him look at me. Watching him lean toward me.

But I am.

I am, and I wait, hoping for something I can't even name but that I know. That I have been waiting for all my life.

He touches me, a feather-light brush of his skin down my arm, a spark I feel even through the roughness of my shirt.

I don't mind being cold, or hungry, or sitting for hours and hours. It is familiar, it is the way things are. But this; the way he talks to me, looks at me, and now, the way he's touching me—those things and the way they fill my heart—

These things I do not know. I just want them.

Want him.

I touch him like he is touching me, tracing my fingers up his arms, resting my hands on his shoulders. His eyes widen, then flutter closed, as if I overwhelm him.

He is so warm. He has steam heat in his rooms, I have heard their hiss and hum, and I can draw the layout of his apartment, his life there, in my sleep.

I can't draw anything now. I am lost, the two of us sliding together, as if the floor was part of a puzzle we needed to lock us together.

"Ava," he says, and then he kisses me.

I don't know how to kiss him back, but I want to, I have seen his mouth in my mind every time I close my eyes, so familiar, so—so gorgeous.

He cups my face in his hands and there are freckles on his face, his nose, a few dotted on his cheeks, and there are gold flecks in his eyes.

"This is crazy," he says, but there is wonder in his voice, gladness and nothing more. He is not afraid of me, he is ready for me, for this.

"Yes," I say, because it is, but I don't pull away. I let a lifetime of planning, of training, go in a moment, a heartbeat, and there is nothing in me that wants to stop.

It is my first kiss and yet it feels like I'm coming home.

"Come downstairs with me," he says afterward.

"Downstairs?"

"Put the—" He points at the recording equipment. "Put it on a loop, play back all the silence it's just heard and come back to my apartment. I want—I think about you there, about you sitting with me. Everywhere I go, I think about you. Want to see you outside this attic." He grins at me. "Have to make sure you're real, don't I?"

I stare at him, shocked. I thought—I could believe he wanted me. That is a simple thing. But this, what he's saying—this I don't understand. You don't invite those who can destroy you into your life. You do not ask them to be part of it. Whatever I feel when I see him, I'm still SAT.

I could destroy him.

Myself.

"Okay, the hall, then," he says, still smiling. "Just come downstairs and stand in the hall with me. Then I won't have to imagine what it would be like to see you there. No one is listening there, right?"

I nod because this is the one room in the entire building where you can speak without your voice being heard by machines that note every syllable and save it forever. I have heard him in the hall, opening his door. I have waited to hear him breathe. I have waited to hear him.

"Then out," he says. "The bar two streets over, at the

end of the block. Come late tonight. The lighting always goes bad then."

Of course it does. All lights do, all the power in the city being turned toward the computer that analyzes every word that was recorded starting then, filing everything away while the rest of the city wheezes darkly, supposedly asleep.

"Tonight?" I say, and my heart is pounding more than it was before, when our skin was pressed together, and I see—I see us sitting together in the sun, our feet in the sand, together, looking out over a wall. It should feel like pretend, but it doesn't, it feels right, and then Morgan leans over and kisses my hands.

I shake my head, trying to clear the images in it out.

But I already know they won't leave.

"You have to go now," I say, frantic, and when he smiles at me, I ignore the way my heart twists, painful joyful scared all at once, and say, "Morgan, you have to go."

Wake up.

26.

"WAKE UP," I hear and come back to myself, to now, gasping, and see I am standing in a shadowed corner of the school, tucked out of sight.

And with me is Morgan. Not in the attic, but here, at the high school.

"What happened? You—you were staring but you didn't seem to see me. Are you all right?" he says, wrapping his hands around mine and I know this, I know his touch.

I know him.

And then I hear Jane saying "Ava? Ava?" her voice rising each time in panic, as if she's afraid I've disappeared.

"We should leave now," Morgan says. "I know a way to get back home. Trust me?"

"No," I say without thinking, but it's true, it's right, the word comes out strong, and his face drains of expression, color, as if I've hit him. As if I've made something inside him bleed away.

"Ava," he says, his face going so pale the freckles on

it stand out sharply, dark brown against chalk white, and Jane's voice comes closer, still saying "Ava?"

They both say the name like they know me, but I don't know myself.

I turn, and see Jane come around the corner. She sees me, sees Morgan, and sucks in a breath.

"You're that—you were at the doctor's the other day," she says, and wraps one hand around my arm, squeezing tight. Pulling me toward her and away from Morgan. "You—what are you doing to my daughter?"

"She isn't yours," Morgan says, and Jane freezes. The two of them stare at each other for a moment and then Jane says, "Ava, we have to go. Now." She starts backing the two of us away, as if he will lunge at us and tear us both to pieces.

Morgan doesn't move. He just watches us go, his shirt fluttering around him in the wind. With my eyes open, awake to here, to everything around me, I can still hear him saying my name. Still see attic walls and him smiling.

Feel my heart race, my own mouth curve as I smile in return.

When he is out of sight, Jane makes us run to her

car, tugging at me until my feet stumble into rhythm with hers.

"Are you all right?" she says when we're inside, locking the doors and then touching my hair, my face. Her hands are cold.

I don't answer, and when the car shudders away, onto the road, I look back but don't see Morgan.

"Turn around," Jane says. "I don't want you—I don't want you to get hurt, Ava."

"There's nothing to see," I say, and when I look at her, her hands are clasped, white-tight, on the steering wheel.

"Yes," she says. "That's right."

But she doesn't sound like she believes it.

27.

JANE IS SO UPSET she goes to the police. I don't want to get out of the car when we get to the station, everything in me freezing at the sight of all those uniformed people walking in and out of the building.

"Ava, honey, we need to go in," she says, and all around us, around me and her and the building, I see another building, almost like it but darker, bleaker, and the people in the uniforms have faces I can't make out but know I don't want to see.

"I'll be better, I promise," I tell her, folding my hands in my lap so she won't see them shake. "Just don't take me in there. Don't give me to them."

"Give you—Ava, what are you talking about?"

"The police, please don't take me there, they keep records and the crèche, I can't go back, please—"

"Ava, honey, I'm not—take a deep breath," she says. "The police help, and there isn't any of that thing you just said. Look, we have to tell them about that boy. I don't want him to hurt you. I want you to be safe."

What are the police here? Not the end of everything? They must be, because Jane seems okay being
here and I—I trust her.

"But I—" I stop.

I don't know how to tell her that I know Morgan
won't hurt me.

I'm not sure I know it. I just—

I know I want to believe it.

In the end, I agree to go in with Jane, and although
at first I see strange, angry shadows through and
around everyone, after a while they go away, replaced
by Jane coming out to check on me every few minutes
while she's off talking to someone and by the candy
bar she bought for me, creamy sweetness melting on
my tongue.

After my third candy bar, this one crunchy and
sweet, Dr. Jabar comes in, looking upset. He and Jane
both come out at the same time, a few minutes later,
but he's the only one who leaves. Jane asks me to come
with her.

"We just need to talk to Don for another few minutes and then we can go," she says.

"Don?"

"The police officer I've been talking to," she says, and Don, when I see him, greets us wearily, nodding at me from behind a desk covered with papers.

"This must be Ava," he says to her, and then looks at me.

"I'm sorry about your accident," he says, his voice very loud. "Would you like to sit down?"

"She's not brain damaged," Jane says, voice sharp. "She's lost her memory."

Don's face turns bright red, and he clears his throat. "Of course. Sorry if I—sorry."

He turns to Jane then, talks to her.

"We still haven't been able to turn up anything on the young man in question," he says. "The good news is, we have a good picture ID based on what the security guards told us. We'll keep looking for him until something pops up."

"Nothing?" Jane says. "His family hasn't reported him missing? I thought he was in the hospital."

"He could have come over from one of the state facilities," Don says. "The paperwork there, it's not so good. And if he doesn't have relatives, that would mean he's probably been moved around quite a bit, and you know how state paperwork—"

"He didn't just come from nowhere," Jane says. "He shouldn't just appear and disappear like that."

"We really are doing all we can. Do you—" Don glances at me. "When you saw this boy at the doctor's office and then again at school, what did he say to you?"

"That he knew me."

Don sighs. "Sadly, that's typical. Do you remember what name he called you?"

Ava. He knew my name. Knows it. Knows me. "Name?"

"Who does he think you are? He probably sees you as someone he knows, and since you aren't that person, what did he call you?"

And I know him.

"Nothing," I say. "He just said he knew me."

"Anything else? Any . . ." Don looks at Jane, who gives him a pointed stare. He turns back to me. "Any threats? Or, er, suggestions?"

"No."

We should leave now.

"Look, is she is danger?" Jane says.

"I don't think so. He's fixated, but it could transfer, and even if it doesn't, he hasn't done anything aggressive," Don says. "We'll certainly keep looking, but overall, I think Ava's safe."

Safe.

How safe can I be when I keep seeing things? Feeling—

Feeling things for someone I'm not even supposed to know.

That doesn't seem to exist here.

I've seen so many strange things, and it all started when I was in the hospital when I saw the old nurse who turned out to be—

Everything in me stills.

"Who called Dr. Jabar?" I say, and Don glances at me, as if he's surprised I remember Dr. Jabar's name.

"He didn't know. He did bring over the message one of his office assistants took about what the caller said, but it wasn't much help. Would you like to see it anyway?"

"Yes," I say, and Jane says, "Ava, I don't think—"

"I do," I say, snapping, and she sits up straighter, no longer looking at Don.

"I have teenagers too," he says, his voice kind, and then I am holding the paper Dr. Jabar brought in.

as i wake

Midway through the description of Morgan, I read, "Cl. states patient is not a danger to self."

"What's this?" I say, pointing at it, and Don looks at the paper. "Clearly states not a danger to self," he says. "You know doctors, always abbreviating things."

I nod, but I'm thinking Cl. Clearly.

Clementine.

28.

I SPENT A SLEEPLESS NIGHT trying to think about Clementine. There are moments—tiny, fleeting fractions of a second—where I almost remember something. Almost know something. *SAT, but now in Science, working on something. Knows everyone. Knows everything. I don't know her but I see her, I see her smile and—*

And that's it. Whatever it is, it stays locked away inside my head, in a place I can't reach, and all I get is a headache, one that makes even the faint night light coming in through Ava's curtains hurt my eyes.

By the time the sun comes up, my head hurts a little less, and all I know is Clementine is definitely strange, and did come by the day I first saw Morgan.

But then, I knew all that before.

Maybe Cl. does just mean clearly. I don't know.

I don't know, I don't know, I don't know. That's the one thing I do know.

And Morgan—

Morgan is part of me, but he isn't even someone anyone here knows?

"Ava?" Jane says, knocking lightly on Ava's door before she comes in and I get up, get dressed. I drag it out, pretending I care which one of Ava's endless array of black shirts I wear, and get to school late, too late to see Greer or Olivia or Sophy.

Sophy finds me before third period though, comes up to me in the hall and says, "There you are! See you out in the garden, right?"

Her smile is mostly teeth. I wonder why she doesn't like Ava and then think of something else, something I see when she turns away and through and around her I see her again, still smiling that same sharp, cruel smile.

Maybe Sophy doesn't like me.

Outside, I listen to the three of them talk. It's like a fight without fists, Greer tossing out words and Sophy taking them on and somehow letting them get to her.

Greer says, "Sophy, come on," and Sophy smiles, sharp, and says, "Come on? That's you, pleading? Better hope Olivia doesn't hear that."

Greer pales and Sophy looks at me. "Ava, you've got crèche taint, and you need to not let that show so much. Get away from Greer."

I don't move. I won't. Sophy is cruel and everything I

hate, everything I've fought against to be here. I stay right next to Greer, who is shaking now, scared.

"Sophy, just relax," Greer says to her. "Me and O still love you, you know. We loved you even when you were, well, you know. Nothing," and when Sophy smiles I realize the one I have seen glimpses of—the other one, the one who is her but not—was never nothing. Never once found herself in a place where she needed someone else. But this one does.

Every—all the mes I am are different. And so are Sophy and Olivia and Greer and Jane.

Sophy says nothing now, but smiles as Olivia leans into Greer, who is fiddling with Olivia's hair, trying to braid it. Smiles more as Greer runs a hand down Olivia's hair without seeming to notice she's doing it.

"How are things with the latest guy?" she says, and Greer flinches, the tiniest bit, and moves her hand away.

I look down at the grass then, smoothing one hand over it. I can't get over how green it is. It doesn't even crunch in my hands when I pull a few strands loose.

The wind blows them back toward me and I close my eyes, feeling them brush against my face.

"Please," Greer says, *"please,"* and I open my eyes to see

her looking at me. She looks different, paler and far more nervous, and her hands are shaking so hard I can see them moving. I know I am seeing a Greer that isn't here but one that—

One that is in my head. One that I remember.

"You can't—shouldn't look so upset," I say and she stares at me, her mouth working.

"I know," she finally says, and then blinks hard, twice. "I just—it's hard. I found a doctor who'd give me some pills, and when I take them things are better. Everything seems so far away." She lowers her voice to a whisper. "Like a dream. I just—they make me a little . . . I don't know. Like I'm not real. I'd like that."

"Greer, you don't mean that."

"I still see Olivia, you know," she says, and her hands are still twitching, shaping the air like she's holding something. Someone. "I see her all the time, even when I'm walking or sitting down to dinner or trying to—trying to work. I see Sophy too and she's here, she's really here and you know Olivia never ever would have helped plot anything. She loved what she did, she loved listening to all those stupid conversations. She shouldn't have been—it was wrong, what they did. Hitting her over and over and all that blood—"

"Stop it," I say, and stand up.

"You were there," she says, and grabs my hand. "You saw what they did to her, how they made us all sit and watch while they asked her what she'd done wrong and she never said anything, didn't ever say what I know they wanted to hear, that we—" She breaks off.

"She kept you alive," I whisper, and turn to smile at the far corner, as if I am just enjoying the view. The day. The park. As if I am not pretending I don't know what Greer is talking about.

"She did," Greer says, and she's crying now, crying in the open, where anyone can see, and I can't stand it, kneel in front of her and pray that there isn't anyone around, or that if they are, they see that Greer is so broken she is no threat to anyone except herself.

"You can't act like you care so much," I say. "You know the rules. Involvement only with approval and only to provide children for the PDR. You and Olivia, if Sophy sees you weak, you know she'll strike and then Olivia will have died for nothing. And she died for yo—" I break off, swallow. To even say what I have just said is to admit I knew what they were to each other. To admit I knew. And I did know.

I knew, and didn't say anything. I looked at them and wondered what it was like to be in love.

"She's dead because of me and I can't bear it," Greer says. "I can't look at myself at this—at this world for another day. I can't—"

"Greer—"

"If I don't disappear myself, Sophy will make sure it happens," she says and nods when she sees my face. "It's true. She told me this morning. And she—she asked about you, Ava. You know not to let her find out anything, right? You know she talks to—"

Greer stops talking and looks around. "Yes, Sophy does work very hard," she says, and then stands up, pushing her hair back from her face and smiling at me.

"I'm sorry, but these cavities of mine are causing me so much pain," she says. "Please don't tell anyone I cried over them." A guy walks by, and I hear the soft whir of a camera clicking, see how he turns slightly toward us. How the second button on his jacket has an extra hole in the middle.

"Hello, Ethan," Greer says, smiling, and he stops, looks fully at us and then blushes bright red, lowering his eyes to the ground.

"I'm sorry," he mouths, glancing at us, and then hunches his shoulders and moves on.

"I hate him," Greer says when he's out of sight, but she's still keeping her voice low again, barely a whisper now.

"He can't help it," I whisper back. *"He's a toy for Kale, who put him here. You know how bad he did in training, how awful his marks were. You saw his face just now. Kale is—it's what he does to live and he's sorry, he really is. Besides, we can't turn our back on what our country needs us for."*

"I've heard you already have, so be careful," Greer says. *"But you—Ava, I think you can."*

"What?"

"You can," she says again, leaning in closer, and her eyes are brighter. Happier.

Here.

"I said, you can wake up," she says, and then turns, says, "I think she's awake now," and I realize I am lying on my back, lying cradled in the green grass.

"You—" I say, staring at the side of her face I can see. "I just saw you—"

"Yeah, you did," she says, looking back at me and smiling. "You just fainted for a second or something.

Oh, sit up, sit up." She nudges me. "Your boy is coming over here. . . . Hi, Ethan."

Ethan? But Greer doesn't even like him anymore, doesn't want to talk to him—

"Hi," Ethan says and Greer likes him fine, waves a hello at him as she moves away, still smiling, still not the sad, lost girl I just saw and I don't—

"Are you all right?" Ethan says, and he is crouching down next to me, one knee touching my shoulder. He has gorgeous deep blue eyes, and I know them. I just saw them when he said he was sorry, only he didn't actually say it. He might have meant it, but he still didn't say it.

But he isn't—he isn't in a jacket with a camera in it, and he's not hunched over but moving easily, grace-fully, sitting down next to me like he knows I want him there.

He seems so happy, but there is something scared in his smile. Not through it, not around it, not in the other him I saw. But here, now, just like how I noticed his smile never reaches his eyes.

It only lasts a second, though, and then it's gone, vanished like everything else I've seen.

But nothing I've seen—none of these moments that

feel so real, that feel like memories, that I know—none of what I've seen is from now. From here.

I squint my eyes closed, battling against the tight throbbing in my head.

"Are you all right?" Ethan asks, touching my shoulder, and I look at him, and then at Sophy.

She's watching us. Staring, really.

"I have to talk to you," I say, and watch her smile.

Ethan watches me get up and walk away like he can't keep his eyes off me but he doesn't like me like that, I know it.

I just don't know how I know it.

I wish my mind wasn't such a patchwork, that it wasn't . . . broken.

"Well," Sophy says, "good way to keep him wondering about you. Nice job."

"I know who you are," I say.

"Yeah, I'm Sophy," she says. "What's wrong with you?"

"I know," I say again and she stares at me like I'm crazy but I'm not. I've seen her—not this her but still her and I know what she can do. What she's done.

"Maybe you should sit down," she says and I jerk my arm away from her when she tries to touch me and she looks surprised but behind it is fury and all around her I see her—*the other her*—standing proud and full of power, and Ethan and Greer and Olivia are here too, looking at me, but I see their other selves too.

I see *everything*, and it's like I'm being pulled in two but no one is pulling me, it's all in my head, my empty head that seems to be full of things I shouldn't know but do and I don't understand this, don't understand me, and who am I?

Who am I, really?

I close my eyes.

29.

WAKE UP.

The chair squeaks as I rock awake, and the attic door opens.

It's Morgan, a bowl of noodles in each hand, and my heart does a little skip-thump dizzy beat.

I want to tell myself it's from the smell of food, but it's not. I know it's not.

He puts one of the bowls on the table that holds all my equipment. On screen, what I last typed is blinking, waiting. "56-412 makes lunch."

"You didn't come to the bar," he says, glancing down at the floor and then back at me. I don't have to guess what he's remembering, because I'm remembering it, too.

I look away, stare at my keyboard. I don't want to tell him that I started to go but was stopped on my way out, pulled back from the brink of whatever I was about to do by the clipped, unfamiliar voice that ordered me to go to the integration office.

I'd gone, terrified for myself—and watched Olivia die.

If anyone knew what I'd done—what I'm doing now,

even—I could be where she was. I have to turn him in, cre-
ate a story to explain away anything he might say.

I have to at least tell him to go and mean it.

I don't say anything.

"Anyway," Morgan says, as if I have spoken, "I had some
extra food, and I figured you might be hungry, so—" He
breaks off, shakes his head, and then puts his bowl down
next to mine. "Why didn't you come? You only live fourteen
streets away."

I stare at him. "You—you've followed me home?" He's
watched when he leaves. I know this because when he leaves
while I'm here, I send in notification, and whatever street
surveillance is nearby watches him.

And now they will have seen him following me. Will
guess that he has figured out who I am. And what if they
find out everything? What if what we did, what I did—

"Ava," he says. "I know how to—I was careful. The
other one, who comes when you leave, has a . . ." He pauses.
"He has a friend come and visit him. They are not always
so quiet, and I have at least an hour to myself."

"I've done nothing wrong," I say, my heart pounding,
thinking of stories I've heard. Of the shattered expression in
Greer's eyes. Of how I couldn't look at Olivia, how I kept
my eyes wide open but turned my mind away. "I told you to

go last time, I did, and I—" I stop, new terror rolling over me. "You know my name."

"You have a card on your buzzer."

"I cleared my crèche status, I can't be judged by just that," I say, still panicked. "I—my buzzer?" I remember sliding the card into the little slot, thinking of the two rooms they claimed, and how they were now my own.

His eyes widen. "The crèche? But that isn't—it's all antigovernment talk. It's not real."

"No, of course it isn't," I say quickly.

"I didn't—I didn't mean to upset you," he says carefully. "I just wanted to see you away from here. Wanted to see you for real. I was careful, I swear. I wouldn't—I don't want anything to happen to you because of me."

I stare at him. He has no apparent beauty, no perfection of features. His mouth is thin, his face is narrow, and his hair is a short, spiky mess, neat only where the dark ends lay flat by his ears and the base of his neck. His eyes are lined with shadows underneath, and shaded with a knowledge that seems to mock everyone, the world and himself. He is thin, too, long fingers and the jut of his elbows visible through the thin fabric of the university shirt he's wearing.

He is nothing to look at, and yet I can't stop looking at him. There is something beautiful in how his face is made, how all the tiny flaws blend together into something more perfect than perfection could ever be.

There is something about the way he looks at me, as if there is something in me worth seeing.

I swallow, and then push up my right sleeve.

He looks at me for a moment, and then moves closer. I watch him see the mark on my wrist, the tiny symbol etched there, the C burned into the skin. I can't remember when it was new and red. For as long as I can remember it's been faded white, a scar.

"Oh," he says, and his voice is quiet. Horror-filled. "But the crèche isn't—it's real?"

I nod. "I was—I was born in it. Lived there until I got lucky and got out, got sent to training."

"I'm sorry," he says, and touches the letter on my skin, gently, so gently.

No one has ever done that. No one has ever touched the scar. No one has ever said they were sorry.

When he picks up one of the bowls of noodles and offers it to me again, I take it. We eat in silence, watching each other the whole time.

I do not write anything about what happened—the food, what he said, what I let him see about me.

I keep it all to myself. A secret, when I know there are

supposed to be none. When I know what they can cost.

I can't sleep that night but I don't go out. I lie in the dark, and when the sun comes up, faint yellow breaking open into the watery gray of day, I get up and eat breakfast, then go for a walk in the park.

I do this every morning, but on my way to the park I can hardly think, I am so tired and frightened. I am scared of what might happen.

I am scared of myself, and what I am hoping.

I sit down on a bench and look at the grass. It is dying. The grass is always dying. It is brought in to the park in long strips from the country, and rolled out and watered. I have heard people bet on how long it will last. Something in the soil here kills it.

The morning watch team comes by, stopping to tie their shoes when they see me. I rub my nose to let them know I've seen nothing and they move on.

Morgan shows up as they leave. I am not surprised when he sits down next to me.

"Are you all right?" he says, and that surprises me.

I fold my hands together so he won't see them shaking and say, "You and I, we shouldn't—"

"Ava," he says, and gives me a tiny, lopsided grin. "You've said that before, you know."

I do. I don't know how, but I do. But I have to say it again.

And I do. "No, I mean you shouldn't—you shouldn't want to talk to me." I look at him. "You know why I'm there, you've always known that. And now you know what I am. Where I come from."

"I wasn't going to talk to you," he says. "At least, that was my plan. I was going to say hello, then grab your equipment and toss it into the street."

I stare at him, horrified. He would die for that and I— well, death would have been a sweet dream for me. "You—"

"I hate what this—" He moves one hand out slightly, just slightly, indicating everything, the park, the whole world. "I hate what all this is. But then—" He shrugs.

"But then what?"

"You said hello back," he says. "I didn't think you would do that." He looks away and then looks back at me, his grin showing again, but slightly bigger this time. "I don't mind you watching me."

I feel my face heat. "I'm not—I don't see you. I'm just listen."

"Is anyone . . ." He trails off, and circles an index finger around slowly.

"No," I say. "No one is listening now."

ELIZABETH SCOTT

"So if I asked you to tell me your real name, would you do it?"

"No," I say, and look straight ahead, at the shriveled grass.

"What if I asked you if you like oranges? Could you tell me that?"

"Yes."

He grins again. "So there's one thing I can ask you, then."

I stand up, and he does too.

"I don't have a name," I say. "I've always been Ava."

"And if there's more than one Ava in the room?"

"There never is," I say. "Ava is a crèche name. As soon as you are given permission to change it, you do."

"You didn't."

"No," I say, "I didn't."

When I walk away, he does not follow me, but when I look back he is still there, looking after me.

The next time I go to the attic—to work, I remind myself on the way there, to work—he is silent for a long time after I get there. I think he is reading, although I am not sure. I report that he is anyway.

"You never asked for permission to change your name, did you?" he says, breaking the silence, and hearing his voice

138

in my ears is a surprise. He almost sounds like he is here, with me.

As if he is talking to me, and I know that he is.

I do not write anything down, and I rewind the last few moments of the recording, noting a glitch, and replace that question with silence.

Later, the attic door opens, and I turn toward it.

"I never asked," I say. "Ava is my crèche name, but it's also my real name. My mother must have—I guess she knew I'd end up there, and so she called me that. It's all . . . it's all I have of her."

He walks toward me, not looking at the equipment, or the papers. He is looking just at me and when he reaches me he sits on the floor, and holds out both hands, curled into fists and facing down.

"Pick one," he says, and as if we are playing a child's game, I do.

He turns the hand I tap over, and opens it. Inside is an orange, small and slightly shriveled, but still bright even in the attic gloom. My vision blurs, eyes burning, and I see Morgan waiting for me, sitting on top of a wall, wearing some strange pants that end at the knees, an orange in hand, a smile on his face. I see him handing me one in the desert, his face gleaming in the sun.

"I—I saw . . . I don't know how to explain it."

"The weird pants? And the desert, with all the sun?"

I nod. "What—what is that?"

"I don't know." But I think we both do and there is a deep, charged silence for a moment. For how we are. For how we see each other and it—we see each other all the way through . . . I don't know.

He clears his throat. "Anyway, I hoped the yes meant yes, you like them," he says, and that's when I know nothing will ever be the same again.

And that I don't care.

30.

WAKE UP.

Everything is gone; the room, the orange, Morgan, and a moment I know. That I remember.

That changed me.

Greer is leaning over me, frowning.

"Wake up," she says and Sophy says, "Her eyes are open, Greer. I don't think you have to keep saying it."

"You fainted again," Greer says, ignoring Sophy and looking at me. "That's twice in something like twenty seconds, Ava. No, wait, maybe you shouldn't sit up."

I do anyway, head spinning, and press my hands to my face to block out the world, to try and figure out what's real and what isn't. What I know and what I don't.

My hands smell like orange.

I start to shake. *Morgan.*

I pull my hands away from my face, and Greer and Olivia and Sophy are watching me, Olivia looking worried, Greer looking worried and a little annoyed. I can't read the expression on Sophy's face at all.

Ethan is standing a little farther away, a blank, almost angry but more resigned light in his eyes that goes softer, kinder as he sees me looking at him. He knows what it's like to be—to be hurt. I know that.

I stand up, shivering, and they all reach for me, all of their hands are reaching for me, and I take a step back and then another and another.

And then I turn around and run.

Once I'm away from school—away from them—I slow down, trying to think as I walk along the road Jane uses to drive me to school. It takes me through neighborhoods full of houses that look just like the one she lives in, a whole tiny universe of sameness, and although I keep expecting to see someone, I don't see anyone.

There's just me.

I take a deep breath, startled to realize I'm still shaking. Whatever happened to me just now has gotten to me, broken past the fragile shell I've built. More than my memory is gone. My soul has wings that beat to a heart I don't understand and I see things, feel things that I know aren't from here, but that are so real.

That are more real than Jane and the life she has made for me.

I turn onto Homeway Lane, onto Ava's street, my street, and see two people standing by Jane's driveway, talking.

One of them is Clementine.

The other is Morgan.

31.

I MOVE WITHOUT THOUGHT, my body dropping to the ground silently as if I've done it a thousand times before, and I roll into the narrow ditch that lines either side of Homeway Lane, ignoring the damp earth smell all around me.

"What did you think I would do, throw you a welcome party?" Clementine says. "You shouldn't be here, Morgan—there's no you here, and I know you know that. I've told you what will happen if you don't leave now. Why won't you listen?"

"What did you do to Ava?" Morgan says.

Silence, and then Clementine sighs. "There was room for her here," she says. "Jane wanted her, and there was space, so—"

"So you just sent her here? Did you even think—?"

"I've thought more than you have, that's for certain," Clementine says. "She fits here, Morgan. She fits, and I made sure that she'd forget before. *Forget you.* Do you understand me? She doesn't know you, and you can't be here. There's no you here. You can't be here, and you'll disappear from everywhere if you stay long enough."

"But you won't?"

"I have someone here," Clementine says. "She's— well, she's not who she could be, but she fits my needs."

"And you've killed her."

"So quick to assume the worst of me," Clementine says, her voice thick with anger and something that sounds almost like sadness. "I wouldn't hurt—"

"Another you? But anyone else, well, that's okay?"

"Ava isn't dead," Clementine snaps. "She's here, isn't she? She's got a new life, a good one. And look, I can't explain everything to you—there isn't enough time— but Morgan, if you go someplace where there is no room for you, where there isn't a you that was or will be, what happens isn't pretty. The universe recognizes wrongness and fixes it. You can feel it, can't you? I know you can. You have to go back."

"Why did you do it?"

"There isn't time for this," Clementine says. "Let me send you home. We'll forget this ever happened. I won't even ask how you figured out how to get here or anything, I swear. And you know I should ask you that. I should tell the SAT you figured it out. Or go to the head of security for the PDM."

"I don't care what you swear or what you want—I want to know why you did it."

"You know why," Clementine says. "It's my job. I take care of problems. And more than that, I would do anything—"

"Send her back."

"She has a life here," Clementine says. "She doesn't know you."

"She does."

"No," Clementine says, her voice weary-sounding. "She doesn't. Go home, Morgan. Go before it's too late."

I hear the sounds of someone walking away, and push myself deeper into the ditch, half expecting to see Clementine peering into it any second.

"You can come out now," Morgan says, and I look up.

The smile on his face makes something deep inside me, something beyond memory, ache.

"You knew I was here?" I say, sitting up, and he nods.

Morgan does look strange, his skin so pale it's almost transparent in the sunlight. But his eyes, when they meet mine, are as dark as memories I didn't think were real until now.

But they were. They are.

I remember another place because that's where I was. Where I'm from.

I remember Morgan because I—the Ava I really am—knows him.

"I—here, I can feel everything you do," he says. "It's how I found you. And I know—I know you're in there, Ava, and I know this—" He points at Jane's house, at the road he's standing on. "I know this doesn't feel right to you."

"No," I say, and it comes out easily, so easily.

So true.

"I knew you'd remember me," Morgan says, and reaches one hand up slowly, carefully, and cups my face, fingers rubbing gently over my jaw. "Clementine thought she'd make you forget but she doesn't know you. You're so strong. So—"

"Morgan," I say, the memories—and they are memories, moments so real I can almost feel them right now, my skin and blood singing so loudly I'm surprised it can't be heard.

He kisses me then and I know him. I would know him anywhere. In a thousand different worlds, as a thousand different Avas, he would always call to my heart.

He pulls away, head tilted as if he is thinking, and without closing my eyes, without doing anything, we aren't standing by Jane's house anymore. We are in a dark bar and he's looking at me the same way, watching me as I cup my hands around a drink.

"Come away with me," he says, his voice so soft I can barely hear it over the quiet, desperate sadness of the bar and everyone sitting in it, holding their own cups and hoping to forget the world for a little while.

"I can't," I say. "If I leave my job, the city, I—they won't kill me if they catch me. They'll take me to the crèche and make me an example. Make me . . . I would wish for death long before it ever came."

"They won't catch us."

"I—this is everything I've worked for. My whole life, this is all I ever wanted."

"And now?"

I circle my hands around my cup tighter. This life was all I ever wanted until now. Until him.

"All right," he says, after a long moment, a moment where I haven't said a word, where I have sat on the screaming want inside me and forced it down. Forced it silent. "I—I should go. I should stop reading books that get people like you sent to watch me. I should go and finish school and be assigned a job and meet a partner the government wants for me and never see you again. I should go and forget you but I can't. I don't want to."

He stands up, sliding on his coat. "I would rather have memories of you than anything else. You—what I feel when I look at you is the most real thing I have ever known."

He walks out. He does not look back. I finish my drink, and then order another one. When I'm done, when I walk outside, I start walking, then turn back around, avoiding the well-lit sidewalk and turning into an alley.

"Hi," Morgan says, and his voice is soft. Glad.

"Hi," I say, and when I reach for him, he meets me half-way.

"Ava," he says, and I am not outside the bar anymore. I am standing on a road, standing by Jane's house, and Morgan is here.

Morgan is with me and I want to go home with him. I want him.

"Let's—" I say, and then a fist flashes out, catching Morgan's jaw, and it's Ethan, Ethan is here.

Morgan falls, crumpling into the ditch. His skin is so pale I think I can almost see the leaves in it through him.

"Morgan?" I say, my voice rising, shaking, and Ethan puts his arms around me, says, "Ava, are you all right?"

"I—Ethan, why are you—?"

"I don't know," he says. His voice is shaking. He looks terrified. "I've never hit anyone before. I just—when you left school, I started feeling worried, and it got worse and worse and I ended up driving over here. I don't know why. I just—I don't know why and if I get in trouble I'll—" He breaks off, his face going into its usual smooth appearance, and then looks into the ditch, looks at Morgan. "Is this the guy your mom is so worried about?"

"Jane? You talked to Jane?"

"She's at the school," he says, blinking a little at how I say "Jane." "They called her right away, and when she got there and started talking I just—I don't now. That's when I left."

"But—" I say, looking at Morgan.

"I know he's dangerous," Ethan says. "Your mom said so. Come on, we'll go get her and call the police. The guy will be out for a while and they'll come and get him and—"

There's a blur of movement, and Morgan springs up, gasping, and pushes past Ethan. He catches my eye as he does, pleading, and I know he wants me to push away too, to run, but for some reason I can't move.

And then he's gone.

"We should definitely go," Ethan says, sounding nervous now, his eyes full of fear that seems to go beyond this, and leads me to a car. He helps me inside, buckling the seat belt around me, and then we are driving away.

I look for Morgan, but don't see him.

Why didn't I go with him? He wanted me to and I wanted to, I did. I felt it. I knew it.

But I didn't.

"My stepfather will be proud of me," Ethan says in the car. "I think so, anyway. Hope so. It's easier—I mean, nicer, when he is." He clears his throat, wipes his hands against the steering wheel, and says "Ava?" as we pull onto the road that leads to the school.

I look at him.

"Are you sure you're all right?" he says. "You just look—I don't know. A little lost."

"Lost?"

"Yeah," he says, glancing at me, and I see another him now, too, one who's sadder looking, worn looking, one who looks at Greer with sorrow in his eyes, who I can tell wishes things were different, better.

Who looks at me the same way.

"I want you to be safe," he says, and I hear it again, from the other Ethan I see through and around this one.

From a memory.

"Be safe," Ethan says, hunching over like always, gray sky glaring down over us, and I smile at him, say, "I'll be fine."

But was I? Am I?

32.

JANE IS WAITING at the school, red-eyed and frightened looking, and as soon as I get out of Ethan's car she rushes over. Her arms feel warm. Familiar, even, in a hazy way that makes me sure of one thing.

There is something in the way Jane holds me that makes me feel loved. Not safe—I don't trust her, not after what I've just heard—but the way she feels about her Ava is written all over her. Given to me so freely, so easily, and I—

I think Jane was once my mother too.

The police come and everyone has to take their turn talking. I hear someone say there's no sign of Morgan. Two patrol cars went looking for him, but it's as if he's vanished. As if he isn't real.

But he is.

When we're finally told we can go, Jane holds my hand all the way to her car. "I know today has been hard," she says when we get in. "And I'm not mad at you for leaving school but I just—I want to know what you were thinking. You know that boy is out there, and—"

"I know a lot of things," I say, and she glances at me, her face turning pale.

"Ava," she says, her voice going quieter, more nervous-sounding.

"I really do remember you," I say, and keep talking even as a smile breaks across her face. "I remember something from when I was really little. You were different. Thinner. Sadder. Broken. And then you were gone."

"I don't—" she says and then pauses. "You must remember something from right after your father died. I was—it was a very hard time for me. I was working two jobs, and you probably saw me leave and were afraid I'd never come back. But I did. I mean, here I am." She smiles at me.

"No," I say as we turn onto Homeway Lane. "You didn't come back. You don't remember what I do because you weren't there. You want me to remember the things you do, but I don't. I can't. You want your Ava, the one who isn't here. The one who isn't me."

Jane stares at me, her mouth open. "I—" she says,

and then pulls into the driveway and parks the car, trembling. "I don't understand what—"

"Yes, you do," I say, and my voice is so tight, so sharp, that she flinches. Then her back straightens and she looks at me.

"You are Ava," she says. "And I'm your mother. And you do not talk to me like this."

"You are my mother," I say, and she gasps in joy, eyes brightening. "Where I—where you took me from—"

"Took you?" Jane says, all the joy draining away from her. Her eyes look haunted. "I didn't—"

"You did," I say. "And where I was, my mother— you—is dead. I'm pretty sure of that, but the rest of my memories have some blanks in them. That and the weird head pain. I guess I have you and Clementine to thank for all of that, don't I?"

"Ava, I don't know what—" Jane says, and then stops. Looks down at her lap for a moment, and then at me.

"Clementine told me she could bring you back," she says. "She said she could make everything exactly like it was."

I don't know what to say. I didn't—I didn't expect

her to say what she just has. To say that what I believe is real. That I am not the Ava who is supposed to be here.

I didn't expect her to tell me the truth.

"It's not, though," I say. "And I—you know that too. I've seen how you act when Clementine is around. How you want her to go. Have you . . ." The next words are harder to say than I thought they would be, which surprises me. "Have you asked her about finding another Ava for you?"

"You are Ava," Jane says, voice cracking, and grabs my hands. I'm not expecting that, and don't pull back in time, feel her fingers wrapping around mine.

It feels real. It feels nice. It feels like something I could know. But I don't remember it, not here, and I know the black hole where my memories are hiding or lost forever will never hold Jane where she wants to be.

"I'm not your Ava, though," I say, and keep my voice as gentle as possible when I see Jane's hurt face. There's no echo of anything through or around it. There's nothing here but her and me and I see that she loves Ava. I see she's sad enough that she could even love me, that she could overlook the things I'd never know, the things I'd do that her Ava never would.

I see that she would do anything for Ava.

I see what happened.

"Your Ava died, didn't she?" I say, and Jane drops my hands and pulls back into herself, arms wrapping around her body. She sits there for a moment, frozen, and then she lets out a small, choked sound. A sob.

"Yes," she says. "I've tried to remember how but I just—I just see your face, see your eyes open but not . . . not seeing anything, and know you're gone. Clementine didn't—she never told me I wouldn't remember what happened to you. She said everything would go back to how it was before, but she didn't say that everything I knew about how you died would vanish, that I would lose those memories."

She looks at me again. "So I know how you feel, Ava. I do. I want to keep you safe but I don't know how. I don't remember what I need to protect you from. I try but there's . . . there's nothing there. I remember everything but the moments that took you away from me."

"You don't know how I feel," I say, my voice rising. "You—you said yes when Clementine said she could bring me here. You said yes even though you knew I wouldn't be your Ava. She was dead and you knew I wasn't her and yet you—"

"She said you knew me!" Jane cries. "She said out of all the other Avas in the thousands of worlds we all walk in, there were always certain people in her life, and I was one of them. That no matter where you were, you would know me, and I would know you."

"So you said yes," I say, trying to keep my voice steady. "You said yes even though she told you that I had another life. My own life."

"She said you needed me," Jane says. "She said you were as alone as I was. I just—you don't know how much I wanted you here with me."

"I think I have a pretty good idea, actually. I'm here after all, aren't I? Here with a head everyone says is empty when it's actually been wiped clean. Clementine did something to me, Jane. She put me here, but I don't belong and I know it. I feel it every day, with every breath I take, and I won't remember what you want me to. I can't. I lost everything—the life that actually belongs to me—to be here, and Clementine didn't do it for you. Don't you see that? She wasn't trying to help you have your Ava back, she was—"

"Oh, God," Jane says, her voice barely a whisper. "She wanted you here. She wanted you here, and I didn't—I heard how eager she was, but I told myself she wanted to help. I see how she looks at you and am afraid she's judging me but she's not, she just—" She presses a shaking hand to her mouth.

"Dumped me here to get rid of me," I say. "Did she—did she tell how to get rid of me if you decided you didn't want me anymore?"

"Get rid of you?" Jane says, staring at me in shock. "I would never—Ava, I shouldn't have wanted you back so badly that I'd do what I did, I know, but I—I do want you here. I want it more than anything. And we—we know each other. You even said you remember me, so—"

"Did she tell you how to do it?" I say, leaning in toward her, letting her see the anger in my eyes. Letting her see that the world I remember in bits and pieces formed me into someone who is not the girl she thinks she knows.

Jane stares at me.

"No," she says after a moment. "And even if she had, wherever you were, Clementine was there and she wanted to hurt you. I don't ever want you hurt, I don't want to . . ." She reaches one hand out toward me and then stops when she sees the look on my face.

"I'm sorry," she says. "I didn't—I didn't know being

here would be like this for you. But I love you, Ava, and I really think we can be a family if—"

"Her," I say. "You love her, you love your memories of her. Not me. You want to save someone who is never, ever going to be here again."

And then I get out of the car. Jane gets out too, and comes after me.

I turn and face her.

"You're Ava, and I love you," she says. "Not wanting me to say it doesn't make it not true. And you—you know me. I know you do."

"But you don't know me," I say, and walk away.

33.

I WALK THROUGH OTHER STREETS Jane
hasn't driven me down every day. They are still carved
with houses, packed so tightly together there are times
when the windows of one seem to almost blur into the
sides of another, but as I walk the houses grow farther
apart, and the sidewalk turns into a narrow, cracked
road that twists by an empty shopping center before
turning into a park, shading dark as the sun sets.

The minute I walk into the park I stop, staring.

I know it. Eyes wide open, looking into the growing dark, I see the same place through and around it,
only it's worn down, the trees naked and stunted, the
grass thin and so bleached of color it almost seems to
shine in the twilight.

I walk down a path, leaves brushing against me, and
behind them, through and all around them, are empty
branches I know. That I remember. They crackle as I
pass, trying to catch me, but I twist away from their
twining grasp.

I sit down on a bench. Here it is solid, wooden and

sturdy, but the ghost of it, the memory I see, shows me one that is crumbling, dried out and withering away.

I hear the sound of someone walking to my right and look toward it. See shadows moving my way, watch as they shape themselves into a person. Into someone I know.

Into Morgan.

"You found the park," he says. "I knew you would." He sits down next to me on the bench, close enough for our legs to touch.

I don't move over. Don't move away.

I want to be by his side. It overwhelms everything else, every other moment that's happened since I woke up in Jane's house.

I can't believe Clementine thought she could wipe this—him, and how I feel—away. He is written in me deeper than memory. He's in my soul.

"I see—I knew a park like this. Know it."

"We used to meet here," Morgan says. "I've waited here every day since I came."

"Why?" I say, and he looks at me.

He doesn't say "for you," but he doesn't have to. It can be left unsaid because I am why he's here.

He's walked through worlds to find me and I move

closer to him, so close our foreheads are touching. He smells strange, like cold, crisp and bitter.

"Clementine said you shouldn't be here," I say. "Was she lying?"

He's silent for a moment, then says, "No."

"So here, you and I, we don't—"

"No," he says again. "And that's why I want you to leave here with me, to go back to where we're both from. I know you can tell something's wrong with me and I'm not—I'm not totally here. This place has no room for me. It might have, once, but if it did it was a long time ago and I—the me I was here didn't live long. And when I breathe, I feel—I feel this place reminding me of that. I feel it wanting me to leave."

"Why did she send me here?"

Morgan looks down at his feet. "I—because of me."

"You?"

He nods. "My parents were—they were well known, once. They had power. She knew them, and after they died—"

"She kept an eye on you. Found out I was listening to you. I remember . . . I remember doing that," I say. "So she found out and—but won't people wonder what happened to me? Won't someone ask . . . ?" I trail off, staring at my hands. Turning them over to look at my palms, my wrists. The clear, unmarked skin there.

"No one will ask because I came from the crèche," I say. "But why didn't she just kill me? Why did she send me here?"

"I don't know," Morgan says, still looking at his feet, and then he looks at me. When he does I gasp because even in the murky dark, the rising moonlight my only guide, I can see how hurt he is. How he hurts for me, for what has happened.

"Ava, I'm so sorry," he says, and I kiss him, I drink his sorrow, I fold him into my arms and it feels right. It feels like coming home. We slip into the dark, onto the grass the night hides, and he pants my name again, his hands hesitant on my skin.

"I won't break," I tell him and I won't, I haven't, I was put here, supposed to be someone else, another me, and I'm not. I know who I am, and I know who he is.

Touching his skin is like reading a book I know, like the dreams I had that weren't dreams at all. His skin is strange, though, cold and stretched tight, and he arches under my touch like he feels it down to the bone, like my fingers can slide inside his skin. Reach his heart.

"We have to go back," he says, pulling away, gasping, and I look down at him, see how the grass, night dark, shines through him, and understand what he's asking. He does not belong here. He cannot stay here. He'll die if he does. He's already fading away.

I lean down, kiss him. The curve of his mouth against mine is so familiar, this place—this here—is nothing, a dream like I first thought it was.

He and I are what's real.

"We have to go back," he says again, cupping my face in his hands. "Please. Just say you want to come back with me. That you want to let go of this place."

"But if I go back, will I end up sent here again? Or worse?"

"No," he says, and kisses my neck. "No, I swear, Ava, we'll be safe. I know who I can trust now and we were out of the city before, we were headed toward the forest, where trees still live and we can hide."

He holds his hands out toward me, waiting, and I want to reach for them, for him.

But I don't.

"I—I think I've forgotten something," I say, staring at him, watching his smile—so familiar, so clear to me, so known and yet there is something in it I don't know, that I'm not seeing. "What is it?"

He looks at me, his eyes huge, and shakes his head, but it's not to say "no." It's something else. It's—

Morgan doesn't want me to see something. Doesn't want me to remember something.

"Hello, Morgan. Ava," I hear, and I know that voice.

I turn and see Clementine looking at us. She's smiling, and I have seen the shape of her smile before. I have seen it echoed in another's face, seen it made into something I thought was gentle. Real.

"I guess I should have known my grandson wouldn't give up," she says, and then I see what I haven't before. I see why she let me live. I see why the curve of her mouth looks so familiar.

It looks like Morgan's.

My grandson, she said.

I want to be asleep and wake up but I already know that won't happen, not here, not now, not to me.

"Ava," Morgan says, but I am moving away from him, scrambling back in shock and fear.

"You didn't tell her," Clementine says, and glances at me before looking back at him. "I suppose I can see why. Habits of a lifetime, and all that. Will you please go home now? She isn't going to come with you, you know. Not after this. Lying, sending her here . . ."

"I didn't—you did this," Morgan says, but his voice is shaking.

"You left me no choice!" Clementine says. "Was I supposed to let you get arrested and taken away to suffer in a rehabilitation institute or worse, end up like your mother and father? I had to watch them die and I won't—I will not watch that happen to you. I couldn't save your mother from herself and her choice of your idiot, free-speech-spewing husband, but I will save you. If you'd just let me help you now—"

"Help me?" Morgan shouts, and his whole body shimmers, rippling pale. "You sent Ava here! We were going to—"

"Run away, I know," Clementine says, and shakes her head when Morgan's mouth opens in soundless surprise. "Did you think I wouldn't find out? Did you really think I'd let you throw away your life to go into hiding with a nothing listener from the crèche?"

"My life isn't yours to—"

"What? Save?" Clementine says. "And for all your plans, you were never totally sure of her, were you? After all, you didn't even tell her about me."

She looks at me. "I bet he told you he was a student and that was it."

She's his grandmother. I think of him looking at his feet. Of him saying I was here because of him. "He said—he said he knew you," I say slowly.

"No, Ava," Clementine says, her voice gentle. "Not here. Where it really mattered. Where you were. He never told you who he really is. Never told you about his family, about me. Did he?"

"I—" I say, and all around and through Clementine I see her as she was, as she is where I used to be.

She touches my arm as I stand in the shadow of a few small, scant trees, waiting. The city shines brightly in the cloudy night behind me.

"Morgan isn't here," she says. "He got a note from you saying you needed to meet him a little later. Your handwriting was easy to copy—you didn't learn a thing until you went into training, did you? Your writing looks just like the print in the textbooks."

I shake my head no, because this can't be happening, it can't be—but it is. Clementine is here, and she is talking about Morgan, and the stories I've heard about her, about what she can do—I have to try and save him.

"It was my idea," I say. "I told him he had to come with me or I'd turn him in."

She smiles at me. It's a gentle smile, and something

about it is strangely familiar. "Morgan's fine," she says. "I wouldn't hurt my own grandson. As for you, I was going to—well, it doesn't matter now. You're not like I thought you'd be, for someone from the crèche, you know."

When I suck in a breath her smile goes gentler still and I can see Morgan's smile in it, I have seen him smile at me like that, with kindness, but he isn't—"Your grandson?"

She nods and then puts one hand on my arm. It's so hot I feel it through my shirt, burning pain against my skin. "You'll want to close your eyes now," she says, and I try to pull away but I can't and my eyes are heavy and everything is spinning, stretching out long and swirling into colors, into nothingness and I don't want to see, I can't see, and close my eyes.

"Good," she says.

I blink, eyes opening again, always opening again, and I'm in the park, in Jane's world, in the world I was sent to and Morgan—I look at him.

"You lied," I say, and he flinches.

"I—yes," he says after a moment. "But Ava, I would never hurt you, not ever. I thought you were safe, I thought she didn't know about you. She was in Science, she was out of SAT, but she—she must have known someone and you—"

I wasn't safe.

And now I'm here.

"You didn't tell me about her," I whisper. "I wasn't safe being with you. I knew that, you knew that, but you didn't—you didn't trust me enough to tell me the truth and now—"

"Ava," he says, reaching for me, but I pull back, pull away, and look at Clementine.

She is looking at Morgan, not at me. This was never about me. Not ever.

And yet here I am. Broken and bleeding on the inside, heartsick, I am here.

Never trusted. No choices.

I turn away and start to run.

I run, and no one comes after me.

I run, and I am alone.

I am in a place where I never asked to be. I am an Ava I'm not.

I run, and there is nowhere for me to go. There are no exits.

There is no out.

I am here, and Morgan—

I run, and don't let myself finish the thought.

I can't.

I run, and everything I know is nothing again.

34.

JANE IS AWAKE when I get to her house—I have nowhere else to go, I can't go back to where I am supposed to be, to the place where I came from, and even if I could, it's clear there's nothing for me there. I am here because of there.

Because I believed in Morgan.

Morgan, who lied to me. I've questioned everyone and everything else, but Morgan . . . I believed him. Believed in him.

Jane lied to me, but at least I saw it.

At least she told me the truth when I asked.

"Ava," she says when I walk in, happy, and I don't understand why. I walked away from her. I made it clear I don't remember this her, or the things she wants. I've made it clear that I'm not her Ava.

She reaches for me and I step away. I want to run again, I want to run forever, but this is the safest place for me, I think.

Safe, with a woman who wants a me that is gone. With a woman who made a deal with Clementine to get me here.

I laugh and it comes out like a sob.

"Something happened to you," Jane says, her smile fading. "Did—" She takes a deep breath. "Clementine came by after you left. Wanted to know where you were. I didn't know—I went looking for you, I went to all the places Ava goes, but you weren't—"

"I wasn't there," I say.

"No," Jane says. "You weren't. She found you though, didn't she? Did she—did she hurt you? I know she's— I know she can do things, but if she hurt you I swear I'll—"

"She didn't touch me," I say, because she didn't. I am whole, I am here. Clementine broke no bones. She just shattered my heart. Broke most of the memories I have. "She . . . she let me in on a few things I'd forgotten. No, that's not it." I laugh that broken sob again. "She told me things I never knew."

"Ava," Jane says, "oh, Ava, honey," and starts to cry.

"You shouldn't be crying," I say, staring at her wet face. "You've got what you wanted. I'm here and I—I've got no choice but to be your Ava."

"There is no 'my Ava,'" she says. "Don't you see that? You are Ava."

"I have one memory of you," I say. "One moment

that you—you, standing right here—weren't even there for. That you won't ever remember."

"But it's a memory," she says. "It's your memory of you and me and if I—if I wasn't there like I am now, I was still—I'm always with you, Ava. You will always—and I am talking to you, Ava, the you that is here now—you are and will always be my daughter. My heart would know you anywhere."

"No, it can't," I say. "It's—it's the kind of thing you want to say, that you want to believe, but it isn't—I know it isn't true. I thought my heart knew things, but what I thought was real turned out to be a lie, and now I don't—"

Jane touches my hand. "I know you're upset," she says. "I know you're hurting."

"You think?" I say, my voice bitter, and then she surprises me. She wraps her arms around me. She hugs me.

I fight her at first. I don't want to be touched by her, by anyone, not again, not ever. I believed in Morgan and the memories I had but they led me here, they've trapped me here, but Jane won't let go. She just holds on, one hand rubbing small circles on my back, a gentle touch, a mother's touch, and I don't remember ever being held like this. Feeling safe like this. I remember feeling loved but Morgan's love led me here, led to Clementine telling me what he hadn't wanted me to see, and before I know it I am crying, strange, harsh sobbing sounds.

Jane says, "It's okay, it's okay" over and over again and even though I don't believe her, I want to. And after a while, I hold her back.

She is smaller than I thought, and when my arms wrap around her, I still don't know her—don't remember her—but yet, somehow, in a way beyond memory, I do. Something in me, in my bruised heart, wakes up, and even though I'm terrified, I don't push the feeling away.

I am so tired of feeling bad. Of feeling lost. Of being alone.

When I'm done crying, my head hurts. Jane walks me to Ava's room, tucks me into Ava's bed. Sits beside me, smoothing my hair.

"You're going to be all right, you're going to be safe," she says as my eyes get heavy, and before they close I realize I want to believe her.

35.

WAKE UP.

I'm in a large gray room with gray walls. Gray light floats in through a grimy window and I scramble out of bed, my breath casting small white clouds that float around me, float away. My feet are so small and my hands, struggling to make up my bed, are small too.

When the bed is done I stand in front of it, stand as straight and tall as I can. While we wait, I stare at the forehead of the girl across from me. I don't know her name. She came in and took over the bed of the last one who died. I remember her because she said she didn't feel well right before she disappeared.

When I feel sick, I never say a word to anyone.

Blink, and I am taller, older, and I am making my narrow gray bed for the last time, ignoring the voices behind and around me as they whisper, "Are you really leaving? Really? How did you do it?"

I did it because I wanted to live. I did it because I wanted out.

I did it because I didn't want to die.

I did it because I want to do something with my life.

I did it because I want to breathe and know that I'm going to live.

That's how I'm leaving the crèche, how I found a way to leave these gray walls behind.

I've been chosen to go to training—it's all I've been told. I didn't ask anything else. I didn't dare. Maybe it was the tests we had to take recently, pages and pages of questions given by a man who looked through us like we weren't there even as he explained what we were supposed to do.

It doesn't matter how I'm leaving. It matters that I am and I will never, ever come back here. I will make that happen, I will make everyone forget where I am from, that I was branded an enemy of the government from the time I was born.

I will be safe.

Blink, and I am sitting on a cold metal chair in a darkened room, a row of faces I can't see in front of me, watching me.

"You're doing very well with your training," one of them says. "Almost done soon, aren't you?"

I nod.

"You never ask about your family," another voice says. "Never asked to see the records of your mother."

"I don't remember her," I say, and force my hands to stay where they are, force myself to stay relaxed, to keep my eyes wide open. Blinking and fidgeting means lying. I know that now.

I am strong.

I will do this. I will become someone.

"You can go, then," the voice says and then I am standing in an empty field, nothing but brown, dead grass as far as the eye can see. No one else is here. No one wants to even walk by this place. See where the dead that don't exist lie.

I lean down and touch the ground. It is cold and the grass is brittle, shredding into nothing under my hand. I pretend there is a breathing heart underneath, that the people who died and were brought here breathe as one, live in some way. That I can sense my mother here.

"Ava," I hear, and look behind me, see Morgan standing at the edge of the field, a white flower, for memory, in his hands.

I am not surprised to see him, but my heart thumps hard and fast all the same, me and Morgan now and forever what I didn't know I even wanted until I first saw him.

I get up and walk toward him and then he is holding me, his arms around me, our fingers wrapped together, holding the flower as one.

"*The lost souls are supposed to be here,*" *he says, looking down at the ground.* "*I never thought about them before. I should have. Ava, I don't care what the government says, I don't care about any of it. I know who you are. I know and I lo—*"

I touch my fingers to his mouth, to silence him, because he can't feel like that about me, no one has ever felt like that about me. It feels familiar, but only with him.

Only with Morgan.

I bend down and put the flower on the ground, put it where the dry grass will break it into pieces, and he bends down next to me too, puts his hands on mine like we are one.

We are one.

He is here, he sees me, and loves—

Wake up.

36.

I SIT UP, startled and gasping, and I am not in that field anymore. I am in bed, Ava's bed, Ava's covers wrapped around me, I was dreaming—remembering— and Morgan—

Morgan is here. I can see him outlined in the dark of Ava's room. He is kneeling by Ava's bed, head bowed, the edge of his hand barely brushing against mine, the most tentative of touches.

I shove him, pushing him away and springing to my feet, crossing to the window, which is open, a breeze blowing the curtains back to show the night sky.

"Ava," he says, his voice scared-sounding, and I hit him as hard as I can, closed fist to the side of his face, furious with him. With myself, for being glad to hear his voice.

For being glad to see him.

"Get out," I say. "Get out and go to Clementine. Go to your family."

"I'm sorry," he says, and he sounds like he means it, his eyes are so sincere in the moonlight, in the faraway glow of starlight, and I think of the dreams—memories—that just came to me, of his hand in mine.

"I should have told you," he says. "But at first, I figured you knew—you were trained, you were a listener, I was your job and I thought—I thought maybe Clementine had sent you and the others as a warning. But when I got to know you, when I—when I wanted to be with you, I knew you didn't know her. And then I found out you were from the crèche, and you told me about your mother, I . . . I was afraid of what you'd think of me if you knew about her."

"You didn't trust me."

He's silent for a long moment.

"I—I was afraid," he finally says. "I was afraid you'd see me as someone who'd hurt you. I was afraid you'd decide to forget all about me."

"And that was supposed to happen, wasn't it?" I say. "Thanks to you and your grandmother, I'm here, where you aren't supposed to be at all. Where you're supposed to be nothing to me. Where I'm supposed to be another me altogether."

"You don't know—you don't know how much I wish I'd told you," he says. "I just—she and I hadn't spoke in so long that I thought Clementine had written me off. Maybe even wanted me gone, when you first showed up. When my parents died, she sent me away to school, and never came to see me, never called me. I never even saw her again until here. But you—Ava, I remember you. I remember you in my soul. Don't you remember me?"

"Yes," I say, my voice soft and when he smiles I say, "So that makes it okay to lie?"

"No. I'm not—I'm telling you why I did what I did, Ava. I can't—do you really think I don't see how wrong I was? That I don't hate what happened? That I have to live with knowing I did this, that I—that she put you here because of me? I would do anything to fix that. Anything."

"So you came here."

He nods, and I look at him. Moonlight shines through him like he isn't even here, casts its light on Ava's carpet.

"You don't have a shadow," I say.

"Not here," he says.

"Why?"

"I—it doesn't matter now."

"Why?" I say again.

"Because there's no me here. Never has been. I came

here to find you because I'm sorry, and because I miss you, because I lo—"

"Don't," I say, my voice shaking. I don't want him to say it and I want him to say it. I want to believe it, and I'm afraid . . .

I'm afraid I will. That I do.

That, in spite of everything, I feel the same way.

He shifts his weight, but the moonlight still cuts through him and no shadow falls where he stands.

"I came here for you," he says after a moment, his voice soft. "I would do anything for you."

"There—there isn't anything you can do," I say. "I remember you, I remember—I remember us—but I also know you lied to me. That . . . all I have left now is what I know. It's all I can trust."

He nods, face somber. "I—you'll never come back with me, will you?"

"No."

He closes his eyes, briefly, and then turns, moves toward the window.

"What, no throwing yourself at me and saying you don't want to live without me?" I say, trying to keep my voice light, but my heart is pounding, pounding.

He stills, and then looks at me. "You might not re-member it," he says, "but you already know it's true."

And then he goes.

I look out into the night, into the dark, until he is a part of it. Until I can't see him anymore.

Then I sit on the floor, in front of the open window, and watch the sky. I watch the sun rise, I watch the stars disappear into the light.

37.

IN THE MORNING Jane tells me I can take a few days off school.

"I think you need a little break," she says as she offers me thick slices of buttered toast, and I nod, thinking of Morgan standing in Ava's room last night saying he was sorry. That he came here for me.

That I was sent here because of him.

I nod because I don't want to face Ava's world—my new world—right now. I want to hide from what I know, what I remember, and what I've learned.

I'm here now, and I have to find a way to live with that. To live here.

So I don't go to school, and spend my days with Jane. She calls in sick to work—"I've always wanted to do that," she says when she gets off the phone after coughing and talking, whispery-raspy about how bad she feels—and we make chocolate chip cookies, which come out burnt; cake, which comes out lopsided; and brownies, which shrivel around the edges but stay liquid and lumpy in the middle.

And it's fun. We puzzle over the recipes—Jane says she doesn't cook much, and I tell her I don't know that I've ever seen a recipe before—and try to figure out things like what the difference between baking powder and baking soda is, and how and why we're supposed to do thing like "sift flour."

"It's like another language," Jane says as we're eating ice cream for dinner and watching a show about famous people talking about how famous they are. "A recipe can't tell you to mix flour and sugar together. It has to say you need to fold them in."

"And then mix, but don't overmix."

"Exactly," she says. "How can you overmix something? And what happens if you do? I didn't see anything about that. Did you?"

I glance at the kitchen, and then at her. She smiles at me.

I smile back.

It's nice, being with her. The littlest things make her happy—me asking her what she wanted to be when she was my age (television star, squashed when she got a summer job at a television station and spent three months getting coffee for people), her taking me shopping and me saying, "Why are you standing out there?" when she starts to wait outside a store when I go in.

It's nice, but at night, every night, I sleep in strange fits and starts, pulled in and out of dreams that aren't dreams at all. The me that was is still there and remembers more all the time.

I remember: *waiting in line for food with Olivia and Greer, Sophy coming up to us and asking to wait with us, the three of us nodding and smiling. Not relaxing until we were done and she'd said good-bye.*

I remember: *sitting with Greer in the park, watching her get up and walk over to Olivia when she comes in, smiling. See her sitting, hands clenched, as Sophy sits across from us in a cafeteria and asks how we are. I remember Ethan, shoulders hunched as he walks into training wearing the kind of quilted winter coat that most people have to wait years to get, how he blushes when Sophy whispers something in his ear, turns a painful, shamed red.*

I remember Morgan.

I remember so much, a million moments; *attic, shadowy bar, field of brittle dying grass. His apartment, all windows and light. My own, small and dark, and how I felt seeing him there, in my rooms, my space. How he touched my face lightly, as if I was something delicate. How he touched*

me, as if I held something he wanted to know. As if I mat-
tered to him.

As if I was—am—will always be—everything to him.

Three days after Morgan came to me at night, three
days after I found out he and Clementine are bound by
blood, I am back at the hospital again, having my own
blood drawn for some follow-up tests. There is still
confusion as to exactly how I lost my memory.

I don't say that I know why, and neither does Jane.
We just head for the fourth floor, for the lab, where we
sit in a small room filled with old magazines and wait
for a long time before I am beckoned back to sit and
have blood drawn out of me, drained into three small
tubes.

Afterward, Jane acts as if I am sick, wrapping an
arm around me as we leave, asking me if I want anything once, twice.

"I'm fine," I say and she says, "Ava, the last time you
had to give blood you almost passed out. Remember
how you had to drink apple juice?"

I don't, of course, and as soon as she says it I see she
knows that too. I see her bite her lip and blink once,
hard. I see her think of her Ava.

"I wouldn't mind some water," I say, and she smiles

at me, and leads me to a drinking fountain like I am made of glass.

In some ways, what she wants from me is enormous and impossible, is about finding someone in me who isn't there and never will be. But in other ways, her want is so small, so easy to please. And simple enough—pleasant enough—for me to do. It is no hardship to have her looking out for me. To want me to be safe, to be happy.

I only ever remember Morgan wanting me to be happy. Morgan—

I push the thought away, push him away, and drink some water, then swear to Jane I will wait right where I am standing while she goes and gets the car.

"You really will wait right here, won't you?" she says, sounding surprised.

"Why wouldn't I? You asked me to."

"I—thank you," she says, and touches my hair hesitantly, gently, before she goes.

I close my eyes when she does, wondering if she ever had a chance to touch my hair like that in another place. A different here.

Nothing comes, no swimming memory that swallows me whole.

And when I open my eyes, I see Clementine standing next to the drinking fountain.

"I need to talk to you," she says. "I—I need your help."

I stare at her, startled. "What?"

"You heard me," she says. "I—look, Ava, Morgan has come to see you, hasn't he?"

"What, you don't know? I thought you knew everything."

"Not here," she says, brittle-voiced. "Has he been to see you or not? I don't—I don't know where he is."

"I don't either."

She pales. "He didn't tell you—of course he didn't, he's so intent on you that he's not thinking," she says, almost muttering to herself, and then looks at me, fierce-eyed.

"Morgan has to go back," she says. "If he doesn't, he'll vanish. And not just here. He'll—he'll be gone everywhere. If you've seen him, you'll—you'll know what I mean. He's—"

"Disappearing," I say, thinking of how the moonlight cut through him when he stood in Ava's room. How he said *It doesn't matter* when I asked him about it.

But it did. It does.

"You have seen him," she says, and for a moment, just a moment, relief is visible on her face.

It terrifies me. Not just because it shows me that Clementine is capable of feeling, but because the thought of Morgan being gone, forever gone—

I don't want to picture it. I don' t even want to think about it.

"You don't want him gone either, do you?" she says. "I see it on your face. Good."

"Stop it," I say, angry that she can read me so easily. That all my attempts to forget Morgan have failed. That I don't want to forget him. "You—you sent me here, you got yourself here, you send him back. I don't know why you—" I break off, staring at her.

"You can't," I say slowly. "You didn't bring him here, and you can't send him back, can you?"

She stares right back at me, and then looks away, stares at the water fountain.

"No," she finally says. "I can't send him back. I've tried but it—it doesn't work. But you—if you would—"

"What, go back with him and then have you send me right back here? Or kill me to make sure this doesn't all happen again?"

"No," she says once more. "No, I wouldn't—"

I laugh, bitter and sharp, and she leans in toward me, her face pinched with anger. I don't have to remember that no one laughs at Clementine. I can tell.

"I don't lie about what I'll do and what I won't do," she says. "If you went back and I sent you here again, he'd just follow you like he has now. And as for you dying—I didn't kill you because I saw you cared about him and now—well, now I wish I had, but if I did, he'd never—he would only try something even more dangerous, try and mess with time . . ."

She shudders. "So, no, I won't hurt you. All you have to do is tell him you won't come back with him. Just . . . just tell him to go. You do that and I'll find a way to make it so this place is the only one you know."

"I don't want anything from you," I say, my voice shaking with fear and anger. She could—and has—crushed my life so easily. "And I told Morgan I wasn't gong to leave with him."

"You have to mean it."

"I meant—"

"No," she says. "You didn't. He—to get here, he had to find you, and he's bound to you in a way I can't unravel, that goes all over, across everything. You think about him still, I can see it, and I know he does the same. That he hopes because of it, and waits. He waits, dying, for you. Do you want that for him? Do you want him to die?"

Dying? I'd seen that he was fading, knew he didn't fit here, and she said he was vanishing, that he'd disappear, but I didn't—I didn't want to believe it was so final. So forever. "He wouldn't—"

"Of course he would," Clementine snaps. "He was ready to throw his life away for you. I tried to stop it, but I only made things worse. To get here and stay, he's destroying himself. He . . . he loves you, and I can't break that. But you—if you find him, tell him he has to go, and mean it, you can. Once he can't feel what brought him here, once you break that link between you that I—how it goes so far I don't know. I wish I'd studied it, but I didn't know about it. But just do this and he'll go back. He won't be able to fight it."

"And he'll live."

"Yes," she says, and I stare at her. He'll live, but I'll never see him again. I'll be here and—

"Look," Clementine says, and points behind me. I don't turn and she half smiles, winter cold, at me.

"Jane's coming," she says. "If Morgan stays, he dies, and if you go back with him, you know I won't rest until he's safe, and he'll never be safe with you as far as I'm concerned. But here—if you're here, just you, you can have a life you'd never have, not even with Morgan. You'll have a real home. You can go to school, to college, have a job you want. You can do—and be—anything here, Ava. Think about that."

38.

I DO.

Clementine watches Jane and I leave, smiling at Jane's bristled, "Are you all right?" to me, at her angry stare that Clementine absorbs like it means nothing to her.

On our way to lunch, Jane asks me if I'm all right at least four times. I say, "I'm fine," each time and think—just for a second—about telling her about Clementine. About everything.

I don't, but there are those moments—those seconds—where I think about it. When I think of Jane as someone the Ava I am can talk to.

Over sandwiches in a restaurant Jane says I love, decorated with pictures of people that the waitress tells me no one knows when I ask, I do think about being here. Really being here.

I don't belong here, but I could. This world is brighter, happier, and in it I have choices. My life has not yet gotten as good as it will ever be. My future has not been mapped out by anyone, and won't be. The choices I make will be mine to make.

I can't quite picture it, even as part of me yearns for it.

"I think I should go back to school," I tell Jane, and take another bite of my sandwich. It is as big as both of my fists put together. I can't believe how easy it is to find food here. How much of it there is.

"That's great! And maybe you'll finally think about taking the SATs?"

"I—I have to join them here? But I—this isn't the same, I thought I wouldn't—" Oh no, no no, I don't want to go through the training again, the tests. The questions. The lights in my eyes.

And then, just like that, no sleeping, no eyes flickering shut, I am in another place.

I am remembering.

I am in the bar where Morgan asked me to meet him, and he is there, sitting across from me. We are together. Hidden in a corner, in the dark of the bar—but together.

"What happened today?" I say, careful to keep my voice normal, but I'm worried. The report I read when I came

in had only a terse notation covering four hours, "56-412, Search," and nothing after.

I don't want to think about how worried I was that Morgan wouldn't come. That he would be gone, taken away. Disappeared by the SAT.

"Search," he says. "I lost most of my books, a pair of boots—they fit the person who took them—and all my food coupons."

"I have food coupons and . . . " And if I give them to him the SAT will know they are mine.

But I'd still do it.

"I'm—it's gone beyond being listened to now," he says. "If anyone sees you with me, or even finds out that we've talked—"

"I don't care," I say, because I don't, I don't care anymore, and he stares at me.

"Ava—"

"I don't care," I say again, and it feels so good to say it. I am sick of hiding how he makes me feel, sick of my gray life and listening to him when I would rather be with him. Sick of pretending everything is the same when it isn't. I know what it's like to wake up in the morning, every morning, with a smile in my heart.

I've never had that before.

He reaches across the tiny table and touches my hand.

"Leave with me," he says, so quietly I almost don't hear him, and when I nod—I don't have to even think about it, I know the answer as soon as he's said the words—the smile that shines on his face makes people stare.

I don't care because his eyes are full of promises. Full of dreams I know we both share.

"Ava, are you all right?" Jane says, and I blink at her, the world I'm in coming back around me, her face and the place we are in turning from shadow to reality.

SAT.

SAT.

I don't want to do that again. Be that. I did it to survive, but I didn't know what it would cost.

"I . . . why do I have to do that all again? I passed the test, the state task anti . . ." I trail off as I see Jane staring at me.

"I—I just remembered something," I say.

"You—did you take the SAT already?"

"No." I hear the shudder in my voice. The SAT—I don't want to talk about it now.

"Okay, well, we can work on that. So, what was it you remembered?" she says, hope in her voice.

A moment when I was happy. A moment when I

decided to change my life. To be who I wanted to be and not who I'd been told I was.

A moment that led me here.

"Nothing," I say, and Jane looks surprised and then hurt.

"But you said . . . oh. It was from—it wasn't about us."

She looks so hurt. I don't know her and she brought me here, she and her want and Clementine—but yet I have seen her face. I know it. I remember it.

It looks just like my mother's. It is my mother's. I know Jane and I don't, I remember her but not her, I remember love and dead grass breaking as I pretended I could feel her all around me. When I wished to see someone I never could, or would, again.

But now I can see her. I do see her.

"It was you," I say softly. "I remembered you."

"You did?" Jane's smile is so alive that the one moment I have of her, the one memory, hurts even more because I never—not until now, not until here—saw her smile like that. Saw her like this, so alive.

"I did," I say. I lie, but it isn't hard to do. This, right now, with her, is real. And I . . .

I like it.

39.

I'M NOT GREETED WITH MANY STARES when I go back to school, the newness of my empty head already worn off, replaced by a pair of pregnant sophomores who turn out to have been dating the same guy.

I don't ask for memories but they still come, showing me the life I was pulled away from. Awake, asleep, they come in bits and pieces all the time now, scattered things like me holding a stub of a pencil and waiting to take a test, me sitting in bare rooms that I know are mine and wondering why they don't mean as much, closing my eyes and listening to Morgan breathe in his apartment as my hands slip under the waistband of my pants because just hearing him makes me want him and the only want I've known is painful, desire to escape, and this—what I have with him, is frightening and wonderful. Overwhelming.

It overwhelms here too. In this place, this now, Morgan haunts me. Rushes through my blood with every beating twitch of my heart.

At school, during lunch, I always sit next to Sophy. Olivia sits next to Greer, watching as Greer reels
boys in and tosses them back, picking one and growing
bored even as they look at her with want-filled eyes.

"Ethan asked about you again today," Greer says
to me after she's told her latest catch, who she already
looks bored with, to go away and give her some space.
"I have to admit, the whole pretending not to notice
him thing works really well—I love it—but you can't
let it go on forever, okay? He's a guy, and they don't
wait that well. Get bored with him before he gets
bored with you, you know?"

Sophy snorts, and then pushes away her barely
touched ham and cheese sandwich when Greer looks
at her.

"Did you say something, Sophy?" Greer says. "Or
did you want to say something? Because I know I'd
love to hear what the never-gone-anywhere-with-a-
guy-and-never-even-been-kissed person has to say."

Olivia giggles, bright and nervous, and says, "Greer,
you're so mean sometimes, I swear," before giving Sophy a small, supportive smile.

Sophy pulls the crust of her sandwich and stares
at Olivia. The hate I see in her eyes makes my breath

catch. Reminds me of what I've seen. What I remember. And even if it was another Sophy, the heart—the soul—is still the same.

Olivia doesn't seem to notice, and maybe the Ava that was wouldn't have seen it either.

But I do.

"Olivia's not—you shouldn't hate her," I whisper, and Sophy stares at me.

When the bell rings, Greer and Olivia head off to class, saying they'll see us later. The moment they're gone, Sophy grabs my arm.

"I know you don't remember how things were, Ava, but you don't—trust me, you don't want to tell me how to feel. You used to—you should remember how they treated us. You should see how they treat us now. How whatever Greer does or wants is okay and we all have to go along with it. I don't know why you won't—you used to get it. You used to say they were making us miserable too and now . . ." She shakes her head.

"Sophy—" I say, and then pause, because she's right. I don't remember, and what I see now doesn't make me feel that Olivia and Greer are a threat of any kind. How can I? They are so clueless, they don't even see they are in love with each other. Or at least Greer doesn't.

"What?" Sophy says, and when I don't say anything right away, she narrows her eyes at me and walks off.

The next day, I catch her looking at me, once, twice, and each time she's staring at me like she looked at Olivia. Like she hates me. Like she wishes I was gone.

I look back at her steadily, my heart pounding, and each time she looks away first.

The Sophy I know—that I remember—wouldn't have done that. She was powerful. Ruthless.

And this one . . . I think this one could be too.

I look through Ava's notebooks that night, scribbles of Ethan's name all over the pages and scrawled messages that I think were between her and Sophy cramped into the sides. "Sick of G and O, A." "Me too." "Wish we could do something." "What, for real?" "Yes." "We can't."

"I could." The hand that wrote that is determined. Angry. Capable of anything.

The hand that wrote that isn't Ava's. I close the notebook and remember how Jane has promised to keep me safe.

I don't think she can. I think I have to.

40.

I AM CAREFUL with Sophy the next day, try to be friendly, but I don't know how to talk about clothes or my hair or the stars of TV shows I don't know, of movies I've never seen.

It doesn't leave us much to talk about, and there is a lot of silence. Stiff, tension-filled silence.

Still, no one but me—and Sophy—seems to notice, and Sophy smiles at me and is perfectly nice, pleasant on the surface and nothing more. I watch her face, listen as Greer says she's "way too nice," meaning she thinks we owe her more smiles, more listening.

I wonder how Greer never seems to get that if you look in Sophy's eyes, anger is what you see.

I see it, though.

I see it, and as we talk in the morning before first period, the four of us is a knot of black clothes that make Olivia look washed out and Greer glow, Sophy seems like nothing, but through and around us standing here we are standing together again, the same but different.

I remember.

Sophy standing tall, standing proud and watching all of us quiver under her gaze. She says, "You might want to turn in more thorough work reports," to me, and just smiles at Olivia and Greer, who smile back, Greer's mouth trembling. Afraid.

I blink, surfacing, and the Greer who is here, the one in this now, smoothes her hair, frowning at me because I'm not paying attention to whatever she's saying. If she would only turn to Olivia, she wouldn't be so needy. She would have all the love and attention she could ever want.

"Well?" Greer says, and I say, "Sorry," because it's expected and because I sort of am. The Greer here does not see Olivia like that, or at least will not admit it. She is too busy making sure everyone sees her to notice the one person who would look at her no matter what. Maybe she is afraid here. Maybe she thinks love makes you weak.

It did me.

I think of Morgan then, my thoughts turning to him so easily; his face, his eyes, his voice, his hands on my skin and how sure I was that my heart knew him rushing over me.

He makes this place, this now, seem like nothing.

"Ava, smile, will you?" Greer says. "Ethan's coming over right now. No, don't look at him, just—"

She breaks off as I look at Ethan, who has walked over to us.

"Hey," he says, smiling at Greer and Olivia and Sophy and then me. His hair falls over his eyes, almost shielding them, but when he looks at me I see them. See the shy, hopeful light in them.

See he does what I do. He is . . . trying to fit in. And he's way better at it than me.

But then, he always was.

"So. Cute." Greer breathes, and Olivia giggles, leaning into her side. Sophy glances at me, and then looks away.

"Hey," I say, because it's clearly expected, and we end up off in our own group of two, Greer and Olivia and Sophy nearby, close enough to watch but not close enough to listen—or so Ethan seems to think as he talks about how he hasn't seen me out in the garden in a while, and the pictures he's taking, which are all of open sky or empty stretches of road.

"I like . . . I like how serene it is," he says. "Can't you just see yourself there, alone and free? I'd love that."

He's smiling and handsome, not pale and fading, his eyes shining openly, brightly, as straightforward as I'll never be.

But he wants to be free, and now I can see what the other Ava saw.

I see that he is beautiful, the dream of what a guy should be, but through and around all that—I see what I know. What I remember.

I see Ethan, his beauty worn down, his voice reduced to short syllables, "I'm sorry," "yes," "no," "I had to."

I see him well-dressed and warm with pain lurking in his eyes as he turns away from Greer's open misery when she and I see him. I see him looking at Sophy with his head bowed, see her smiling at him as if they aren't equals, but as if she owns him.

I see him pale and sad, his eyes full of sorrow.

I see all that and so the Ethan here, the shiny, smiling guy who loves photos of lonely, empty spaces and wants to talk to Ava badly enough to have all her friends listen to him, is muted. Seems like a shadow.

"You're really . . . you're different now," he says, but his voice is playful, waiting for me to say "How?" and smile, be the mystery girl, the one with the lost memories but who still fits into this world.

Be the Ava who was.

"How?" I say, but don't smile because I can't. I can't because I can't tell him that I know him, that I have seen him, and that he is miserable, that he has everything he wants but belongs to someone else, body and soul. I can't say that I have seen him struggle to keep a tiny bit of himself alive and that he is failing, falling apart.

"You're more serious," he says. "I like that." He pushes his hair back, uncovering his eyes, and although he's still smiling, there is something in his eyes—a sadness—that catches me. Makes me still.

"Are you all right?" I say, and I am gone again, am with him in the cold park.

"Are you all right?" I say, fighting to keep my teeth from chattering and he shakes his head, says, "I'm fine, Ava, just fine," and pulls his new coat tightly around him, flinching when he sees me notice it, says, "I have to. I'm not—you did okay on your exams. I didn't. And Kale is . . . he looks out for me."

"PDM?"

He nods. "He works in defense. He actually met Clementine, the woman who is the Science Division, once. He says . . ." He trails off.

"Ethan—"

"I had to go with Kale," he said. "I didn't—you know what they do if you don't pass the SAT tests? I don't . . . I want to die, but I don't." He shivers again. "I'm fine, for real, okay?"

"I'm fine," he said, and says it again now, but now he seems to mean it, the dark light in his eyes fading away. This Ethan is alive and kind and I wish I could like him, but I can't.

I can't because my head—my heart—is still full of Morgan. He is the only bright spot in my memories, in the life I had. I felt like I was someone—not a crèche girl, not an experiment to see if the damned could be saved, but just a person, just me—with him. And that—

That was—is—everything.

Morgan talked to me like I was his equal. Like we were the same. Like I mattered, and past the first rush of him knowing I was listening and him seeing it, wanting to understand it, wanting to be inside it, subvert it, he saw me. He could have come once, twice, and left. But he kept coming back.

He came back for me.

Then—and now.

"Ava?" he says, but it's not him, it's Ethan, and we are still in school, still in this bright shiny world of plenty. I am here, I have this life now, in this place, and Morgan—

Morgan will die if he stays. If I don't make him go.

The bell rings, stopping whatever Ethan was going to say, and I avoid him and Greer and Olivia and Sophy for the rest of the day, thinking of Morgan.

Thinking of what I have to do.

That night, I lie awake in Ava's bed until the stars are high and bright in the sky. And then I get up and walk downstairs just like I did that first night. I walk outside, onto the road, just like I did that first night.

But I don't wonder where I am. I don't wonder who I am. I know that—I know all of it now, or at least know enough to understand what I have to do.

"Morgan," I say, barely a whisper because I don't want to break the silence, the night, I don't want—

"Ava," he says, and I close my eyes.

I don't want to do what I'm going to, but I have to do it. I don't—I would rather stay here, alone with only my memories than have him die. I can't—

I can't bear the thought of that. I can't—he can't die because of me.

I open my eyes.

I look at him.

41.

MORGAN LOOKS LIKE A GHOST, the dark only highlighting what was hinted at when I saw him before. He's faded around the edges, as if his face and hair and arms and legs have been smoothed into the air around him. As if he's being erased.

"It's not as bad as it looks," he says, and smiles at me, a wry twist of his mouth that I remember. That I love. I want to think *loved*, but it isn't past. It isn't gone. My heart still knows him.

I would know him anywhere. Would love him anywhere. And in the world I knew, the one we lived in, the one I remember, he might have told me the truth of who his family was one day. He might have made the choice to tell me.

He might not have. I don't know. I can't know. I'll never know, but now I understand why Morgan didn't tell me. I understand his fear. I feel it.

Now I have to make my own choice and it's—

I don't want to make it. I don't want him to go.

I take a deep breath, then another. It still hurts,

deep down in my chest, in my heart, when I speak.

"You can't stay here," I say.

"But you're here," he says, as if that's all that matters, as if I don't see what's happening to him. As if he doesn't want to see it.

"Do you . . . do you know who told Clementine about me? Who sent her to find me when you and I—?" I say and then stop, because I know the answer. I see it in the ghostly shimmer that marks where solid skin of his shoulders should be.

I see it because he's here.

"No," he says. "I've asked her, but she says she'll only tell me after I go back. When I can't—when I won't be here. I wish . . . if I could do it again, I'd tell you about her, I swear. If I had, you wouldn't be here."

He shoves his hands in his pockets and blows out a breath. "You might not have wanted to be with me but I—at least you would still be there. I can't . . . I can't live in a world that doesn't have you in it. I don't want to live—"

"Stop," I say, my whole body shaking. "I'm not—no one is worth this, what you're doing."

"Ava—"

"I wouldn't do it for you," I say, and the words come

out strong and clear, echo into the night. Sound almost true, even though they aren't.

"You have," he says. "You could have turned me in a dozen times or more, starting from the first time we met, but you didn't. You wanted to be with me. I wanted—I want—to be with you. This place—I see the beauty in it. The warmth. But I can't feel it, and I don't . . . even if I could fit in here, I wouldn't want to. It's not—it's not home. Don't you feel that too?"

I shake my head but I do feel it, I have felt it with every breath I've taken since I woke up in a bed I didn't know, found myself in a place where I belonged but was not—and can never be—from.

"Liar," he says, and when I look at him, he's grinning, a smile I know, that makes my blood sing inside me, every beat of my heart reminding me of what I know. What I remember. How the only happiness I've ever known—the only real happiness—was with him.

I look at him, and he is so pale. So close to disappearing. To death. He would die for me.

And he will, if he stays.

"I don't—it's not easy for me here," I say, careful to keep my voice steady. To not show how much each word costs me. "But I could fit in. I could be something more than I ever was before. Be someone. I know you're sorry about everything, and I—we—lived in a place where trust wasn't easily given. I understand why you didn't tell me about Clementine, I do, but I don't—I don't want to go back. I don't want you."

He stares at me, and his eyes are full of memories I know, that we share. The world we lived in and more and more and more beyond. Forever. Always.

His eyes are full of love, and I see, finally, that he didn't tell me about Clementine because he didn't think he had a choice. He knew who I was, he knew where I'd been, where I'd come from. He'd known I'd see Clementine's power and be afraid. So he made his choice, and when it sent me here, he came.

He loved me—loves me—enough to be here now. He came, waiting and hoping for me to remember my life, remember him. He came here, hoping I'd understand.

He's dying just to say he is sorry.

"Go home," I say, my voice sharp, and I want him to, I do, because I don't want him to die. Not ever and not—not over me. Not because of me.

"Come with me," he says softly, and takes a step toward me. When he touches my hands I know I should pull away but I can't. Just this once, just for this moment, let me—

I can see my hands through his.

I pull mine away, curl my fingers into my palms, digging my nails into my skin. Force myself to look at him.

"No," I say. "I'm here and if we go back, Clementine will—she'll still be there. We won't be safe, not ever. What we had is . . . it's gone."

"Gone?" he says. "We're forever, Ava. Don't you remember how we both saw—"

"Stop," I say, but my voice is shaking.

"If we go back, it would be different. I know it would be. I would do anything—"

I take a deep breath. I close my heart.

It hurts.

"Then listen to me," I say. "I can have—I do have a future here. A real one. Go back and let me—let me have that."

He looks away from me then, stares at the road I saw when I woke up and didn't know where I was.

"This is what you want? Where you want to be?"

"It's where I am," I say. "I can't live in my memories

anymore. I can't—I don't want you haunting me."

"Ava," he says, and I shake my head, saying "no" without words because if he says anything else I will break, I will beg him to stay, or I will go with him, and I do not want to be that weak.

I don't want him to die. I don't want to go back and have this happen once more.

I don't think I'm strong enough to send him away again.

I never knew what love was until Morgan, and he shouldn't die for that. Loving Morgan means letting him go. Love—real love—can't be defined. It just is.

It just lives in your heart, like he lives in mine.

"Go," I say, and this time, finally, I mean it. I want Morgan to live more than anything else. I want it more than the pain of my own heart, breaking.

"You—you mean it," he says, and his voice is barely a stunned, broken whisper.

I don't have to say yes. I just walk away from him. I walk back to Jane's house. To the room that is mine now. To the life that waits for me.

I think I hear him say my name, once, but I don't look back. I keep walking.

Inside Ava's room—my room, now, I have to think my room—I climb into bed. I close my eyes. All I see is him.

I get up and walk over to the window. I look out at the road.

It's empty now.

"Morgan," I say, a whisper, and then again, louder. "Morgan."

There is no answer, and I know there won't be anymore.

Morgan is gone. He'll be safe now. He'll live.

I'll never see him again.

I don't cry. I can't. It hurts too much, and I'm afraid that if I start, I'll never stop.

42.

MORGAN IS GONE, and now Clementine is too.

Jane is the one who tells me, says she heard Clementine moved away two nights after I told Morgan to go.

"Moved?" I say, and Jane nods.

"Apparently she called the hospital and said she'd bought a home in some retirement community out West, and was leaving right away." She pauses for a moment. "Is she—is she gone for real? Back to where—?"

I nod. Neither of us finish Jane's sentence, say "Where she was from." Where I used to be.

"Did you—did you see her before she went?" Jane says after a long moment, and I look at her.

"I heard you . . . you went out the other night," she says. "And when you came back you looked . . ."

She stops then, and I know why. I'd looked nothing like her Ava then. I'd looked broken in a way she doesn't understand.

"I didn't see her," I say.

Jane nods, and tentatively reaches for me, touching

her hands to mine. "Are you . . . are you all right?"

No. A thousand, a million, a billion times no.

But I am here, and Jane—I don't remember this Jane, but I remember another one and Clementine knew what she was doing when she sent me here. I feel a connection to Jane. I had a mother, once, briefly, and it was Jane. And now, here, she's in my life. Wants to be with me.

"I'm fine," I tell her, and am rewarded with a happy smile, with Jane's joy. And it—it doesn't make me into the Ava that was here but it—I like seeing Jane happy.

I like knowing I can do that.

It could be enough, maybe, or at least a start, but the problem is that at night I tumble into dreams that aren't dreams at all. I tumble into memories and wake up aching for a dying world and a quiet, cold life that offered me nothing but sitting in a still room.

I wake up and think of Morgan, who is gone.

Who I sent away.

I like Jane, I do, but I am tired of her Ava's life, of the routine of school and friends who say and do things that are beyond my understanding. I am tired of watching Greer and wondering why she doesn't see what is obvious, wonder why she can't see happiness waiting for her with Olivia.

I am tired of Sophy and how her barely hidden rage makes my skin crawl. I am sure she did something that led Jane's Ava to harm now, but I cannot figure out how she did it.

I'm not worried about stopping it, though. This Sophy is nothing like the one I remember, wears her longing for power so strongly I am surprised no one else sees it. But then, this place is so much about how things look, and not how they are.

Morgan would be nothing here, would be seen and ranked as "average" by Greer and Olivia, would disappear into the school, the world that is supposed to be mine. No one would see the sly humor in his eyes, his smile. No one would see that he watches the world and understands it even as he can see past it.

No one would notice the freckles sprinkled across his face, dotting his nose and his cheeks, and want to kiss them like I do.

Did. I did. I don't want to do that anymore.

I can't.

That night, I lie in Ava's bed and look out her win-

ELIZABETH SCOTT

dow. There is a gap between the top of her curtains and the glass, a gap where the stars shine through. I lie there and watch them.

I am used to not sleeping now. I was used to it before only I don't—won't—ever wake up to see Morgan and—

Push it away, push it away. He is safe now, and so am I.

I yawn and feel my eyes grow heavy. I roll onto my side and close my eyes. I pretend Morgan's face is not all I see as I drift off to sleep, but it is.

I think it always will be.

43.

WAKE UP.

I do, gasping, but for once I'm not in a dream that's a memory, I'm here, in this place, but I feel—

My skin feels tight, my throat feels tight, I can't get enough air, I am not the Ava I am supposed to be and something knows this, is calling me.

Someone.

I get up and look out the window, dread pouring over me, filing me up.

I see Clementine. She is standing on the lawn, standing right where I took my first steps out of Jane's house.

She is standing there, and she is waiting for me.

I move out of Ava's room quietly, slip downstairs and outside.

Clementine doesn't look surprised to see me. She doesn't look like much of anything. She looks worn out, drained.

"Thank you," she says before I can say anything. "I—I wanted to make sure Morgan went home and you did that. He . . . I can't feel him here anymore. Can you?"

"No," I say, and she almost smiles at the anger in my voice.

But only almost.

I stare at her and she looks away, stares up at Jane's dark bedroom windows. "It's funny. I promised her I could bring her daughter back and I did, in a way. You fought me, you know. You—I put safeguards in place. Your memory was supposed to be gone and I even made it so you'd get headaches if you did remember anything. But you kept going. All of this—I did all this for Morgan, and I'll never see him again."

"He's safe, then?" I say, meaning that he's away from her, he's free, and she looks at me then, sees what I mean.

"He's more than safe, and no, I'm not sorry for what I did," she says after a moment, her smile all teeth, and shifts her weight from one foot to another, making all of her blur for a moment, not like Morgan's pale fading but something stronger, something that makes all of her vanish for a split second. "He's alive. He's alive and he—he'll be fine. He'll forget you, I know it."

I stare at her smile, start to say something, and then see how pale she is. How faded.

No shadow.

"Yes," Clementine says. "It's happening to me too. I didn't—my anchor died on me, you see. The Clementine here, who I kept so safe, who I made sure would sleep through all of this . . . she's gone. Her heart stopped. Weak. I didn't expect that, and now I'm stuck here. I thought I had it all figured out. I could come, I'd make sure the Clementine here was sedated so I could stay for a while. I just—all those years around death, watching my daughter throw herself away for what she thought was freedom, seeing her and her husband die, trying to keep an eye on Morgan while keeping my own head because I was sure I could find a way to make sure anyone dangerous could be sent somewhere else because there are always variations of where we are that need us. All that, and now—"

She laughs, a soft sound that is like a sob. "But I never thought about what would happen if I went to a place where I was, or would be, and the me who was or would be died. I ran tests. I've never died before and I've been in worlds—" She shakes her head.

"I never thought—I only thought about doing what I had to, and then going. But this self tied herself to me just like I did, didn't she? I didn't see—I never saw that if you went into a place where you already were, you had to deal with being two. Is that—is this how it is for you?"

"I—"

She shivers, and I fall silent. "I can feel all of them, all the versions of me I've seen and they—they're calling me. I can't hear anything but them. There are so many. I didn't realize what I was doing. I should have thought about it more, but I wanted to stay alive. I'd gone from Security to Science. I was so close to dying myself and I wasn't—well, I didn't want to."

She closes her eyes.

"That's better," she says. "It's not you I don't want to see, although that was always the idea. But now I just don't want to see this place. I can't believe—of all the places to die, this one?"

She shakes her head, and opens her eyes. "I didn't think you'd do it, you know. But you really do love him. You never would have turned him in, would you?"

"No," I say. "I wouldn't have done that."

"How do you know?" she says. "How do you know what's really in your own heart?"

"I know," I say, my voice strong, and it's true. All I

have now is my heart, and in every memory I have, in everything I know, I never once thought of Morgan as I was supposed to. He was never a number, never what he was supposed to be. I was afraid of it, intrigued by it—and him—and then lost my heart. And I lost it willingly. Gladly.

It has always been his and I broke it so he could live.

"You should have—if only you hadn't been assigned to Morgan," she says. "You are so loyal in the wrong way for—well, I suppose that's why it was so easy for me to send you here. All I had to do was tell you he'd sent me to find you. To help you. That all you had to do was to take my hand and close your eyes."

"That's how you—that's how it happened?"

She nods. "You were scared, and I knew—well, I knew who you were. I knew you had to go. So here you are. And now here I am. I—I'm almost sorry, Ava."

I take a step toward her.

"Send me back," I say, pleading, my voice cracking, and she shakes her head.

"I—even if I wanted to, which I don't, I can't. Everything is—" She closes her eyes again. "I can't stop hearing them, all of the people I am—so many, desert, ocean, palaces, stars—and it—no. I can't. It hurts, just being here. Just breathing. I don't know how Morgan stood it."

"He's better than you."

"Don't be so obvious," she says, and then opens her eyes, looks up at the sky. "But you're right. He is. And I—I can see why he loves you now. "

"Who told you about me?" I say. "About us. At least tell me that. Just—"

"That, I would do," she says. "But I don't remember now. All I can still see is you there, waiting. I can still remember knowing I'd save Morgan, but the rest—it's all fading."

She smiles at me then, a real smile, sweet and true, and I see Morgan in that smile.

I think about Morgan then; I miss him, and nothing will change that, not ever, and then Clementine shudders again, her whole body shaking, and turns away, walking off into the night.

She doesn't look back, doesn't say anything else.

Doesn't say she's sorry.

44.

CLEMENTINE'S FOUND DEAD in the morning. It makes the *Wake Up!* morning news because the person who finds the body, a neighbor who stopped by when she saw the front door open, swears the body she saw looked like it had died weeks ago, but Clementine had just talked to people at the hospital about moving. Been seen there a few days before that.

And, if that wasn't enough, the neighbor is sure that she saw two bodies for a moment, the long dead one and another, a "twin," two bodies somehow twisted together, both of their mouths open in unheard screams.

The neighbor is currently in the hospital "under observation." Seeing a dead body is hard for anyone, the doctor interviewed on television says. "The mind plays tricks," he adds. "It will see things that aren't there in an attempt to cope."

"It's—it's hard to believe she's really gone," Jane says as she turns off the TV. "And poor Mrs. Dean, finding her that way . . . There are friends—were friends. No wonder she saw things that weren't there." Her voice is hesitant on the last words, uncertain.

"You think?" I say.

Jane looks at me.

"No," she finally says. "I'm sure that—I'm sure there were things in that house that no one should see. But it's over now, Ava, it's really over. Clementine can't—I know she hurt you, but she can't anymore."

Jane's right about that. I think of how I asked Clementine who had told her about me and Morgan, and how she'd forgotten.

How she said she didn't remember how to send me home.

How that, even if she did, she wouldn't.

"It is over," I say, and Jane frowns a little and touches my hands.

"It's okay now," she says. "You and me, we're safe. We—"

"I'm never going to remember what your Ava knew, you know." I say. "Clementine lied to you about that. She didn't . . . she didn't bring me here for you."

"I know, but you are here," Jane says. "And you shouldn't say—there isn't a 'my Ava' and you. There's just Ava. Just you." She twines my fingers in hers, not tightly, but gently, loosely. With love. "I know you didn't ask to be here but is it—is it so bad?"

"No," I say, and let my fingers twine with hers because it isn't, not in the way Jane means. I have everything I could ever want: family, food, shelter, and a chance to decide who I want to be, what I want to do.

"Thank you," Jane says, her voice full of joy, cracking with it. "And now, I think . . . I think that if you don't want to go see your doctors anymore, if you want to just start over, it's all right with me. I believe—I know this is my—our—second chance, and I think we should take it."

"No more doctors?" No more watching Jane try not to hope when I take tests and peer into lights and have magnets or radiation beamed around and in my head.

No more trying for what we both know can't ever be.

"No more doctors," Jane echoes. "Just you and me. How does that sound?" There is so much hope in her voice, in her eyes, in her shaking smile, that I can't stop looking at it.

She loves her Ava too, and always will, but she sees me too, and wants me here. I see that now.

I see that she loves me—the Ava I am. I look at her and finally see myself in her. I see where the love I had in my heart to give, the longing that led me to Morgan, to leaving all I thought I wanted behind, came from.

I see who loved me first, before anyone else. I remember a Jane who was different, drained and lost. But I see this one can be with me. That she wants to be. And I can be with her.

"You and me," I say, but even now, seeing how much she loves me, and feeling it, understanding it, I still can't bring myself to say "Mom."

I still don't—I still think about what I had. Who I've lost.

I still think about the mother I never got to have. I still think about Morgan, and dream of moments that aren't dreams at all. I dream of my life, and I can't go back it. It will only ever live in my head now. I had so little, and my choices were so small. But I had them, and I made them. They were mine.

"Oh, Ava," Jane says, and kisses the top of my head. She smiles at me with so much love that I can almost believe it will be enough, that I will learn to belong here, that I will become yet another Ava, that I will turn into someone new.

I could be happy here. Maybe all I have to do is try.

Maybe that's all it takes.

It isn't.

Or at least, it isn't at school with Greer and Olivia and Sophy. They take one look at me when I show up, still smiling from talking to Jane, and gather together, motioning me over.

"Enough is enough," Greer says. "It's the weekend, finally, and you haven't done anything with us for ages, so tonight's the night, Ava. You know what I mean, right?"

She shoots me a sharp-eyed look, all meaning that slides through me because while I know it's about things that the other Ava understood and wanted, they aren't what I want. I am the same age as this Greer, but I feel so much older.

I have seen more, lived more, than she ever will, I think.

"Greer, don't be mean, you know Ava doesn't—she doesn't remember anything still," Olivia says, giving me a gentle smile. "Is it really awful?"

"No," I say, and Olivia blinks and then yawns, stretching her arm up over her head and showing a pale strip of skin that Greer looks at and then turns away, snarl-smiling—her version of interest—at a boy passing by.

Olivia's face drops, but she keeps talking. "Anyway, tonight," she says, "we're going to Brent's party."

"And we're going for you, Ava," Greer says, having gotten the boy's interest and already gotten bored with it. "We heard Ethan's going to be there and it's time you started . . ." She gestures at my head. "You need to be more than that girl with no memory. You can at least start on making someone, anyway."

"And Ethan did ask if you were coming," Sophy says, and Greer says, "I think we've all already figured the reason why for that one out already."

Sophy smiles, teeth clenched, and nods.

"I'm glad you're coming with us," Olivia says to me, her heart-shaped face lighting up as she glances quickly at Greer. "It'll be fun."

Sophy's smile goes sharp, and I know it. I *know* it. "It will be fun," she says. "I mean, usually, we just all sit around and watch Greer go for some guy that she ends up doing nothing with, don't we? It's like—I don't know. Do you maybe like someone you don't want to tell us about, Greer?"

Greer ignores her—ignores us all—moving back toward the boy she just cast away, talking to him in a low voice and then laughing, head thrown back so her dark hair ripples down her back.

"I gotta go," Sophy says, and walks off, her steps so careful I know she's about to explode from all the fury inside her. I wonder if she's more dangerous now than she was as I know her. No, knew her. Has to be *knew* her, now.

"Is Sophy okay?" Olivia says and when I look at her, Olivia's normal, sweet smile is gone, replaced by a weary, scared-looking frown. She looks away and I follow her gaze, see Sophy looking at us. Staring at Greer, hate in her eye.

The Sophy I knew wouldn't have been so obvious. But this one is, and her intent—her longing to be someone, to have power—is so clear. I don't know exactly what happened to the other Ava, but I do know this—I'm safe here now. I know Sophy, her true heart, and she can't hurt me.

From now on, I can—and will—write my own future. I have to.

I think of Morgan in class, dream of him awake and with my eyes wide open, but tell myself to let it go. To let him go.

It's hard, though, because they aren't dreams. They are memories, they are what I know: his skin, his voice, the way his hand felt in mine, how his fingers would skate over the calluses life in the crèche had left on me as if he wanted to know them, as if nothing about me could push him away. I remember him kneeling in front of me, eyes bright, hands behind his head, and the steady spark thump that burned through me.

I remember standing in the dark with him, staring at the stars and knowing that I was outside the city, away. Free.

I remember that and it's gone—it was taken from me—and at lunch, sitting across from Sophy, I see who told Clementine about me and Morgan. It's so obvious now.

Sophy wanted power, she always did. She still does. She had it there, where I lived, but she wanted more, and Morgan and I—knowing about that would have given her access to Clementine, so worried about Morgan. It would have given her even more power. She broke Greer. She made her and me and Ethan—everyone—watch Olivia die, just because she could.

Whispering about me into Clementine's ear would have been nothing to her.

She broke me once.

She won't break me now. I survived the crèche. I can survive this, easy.

I tell the three of them I can't wait for the party. I ask Sophy to pick me up.

"If you can, I mean," I say, and she nods, hiding her smile until she looks down at her food. But I see it.

I'm ready for it. For her.

45.

JANE IS SURPRISINGLY HAPPY that I'm going out, although she wants to know where I'm going and what time I'll be home and it reminds me, for a moment, of standing stiffly in a room, and reciting details of my life to someone who sat, already knowing my story and never once looking at me. Just testing me, to make sure I was still worthy. That the crèche girl wasn't falling apart.

I shake my head and Jane says, "I'm sorry, but you have to tell me where you'll be, and you have to be back by midnight. It's a rule in this house, and it's not changing." She says it with ease, as if she's said it dozens of times before and for a moment, I get a glimpse of what her Ava was like.

Her Ava wouldn't have quietly answered the person who wrote down what I was required to say like I did to survive. She would have pointed out that everything about her was known, that her life would barely be her own once she was done with training. She might have even said what I always felt, gave voice to the humiliation of it all. The anger.

That girl, that Ava, didn't live here. She wouldn't have survived the life I had. She could talk, sure.

But she died.

I smile at Jane. "I'm going to a party with Sophy and Greer and Olivia," I say, feeling a sudden rush of tenderness for her, who just wants to be in my life. Who already holds me in her heart.

"Really?" Jane says. "That's . . . oh, Ava, I'm so glad you're doing things with your friends again. Not that I want you to do *things*, but you know what I mean." She throws her arms around me, squeezing tight, and I hear her sniffle once. "You seem happier now. Are you happier?"

"I have choices here," I say, and she sighs, quickly and sadly at my non-answer, but when she pulls back to look at me she is smiling.

"You do have choices," she says. "You have—you have your whole life ahead of you and Ava, you're going to be—I know you're going to do amazing things. And you—" She looks down at the floor. "You'll always have me. Always."

I wonder what that will be like, a lifetime of having Jane in my life. Will we ever fit together like she wants us to? Can we?

I kiss her cheek, touched by her belief, and she looks up at me, her eyes bright and happy.

"We're getting there," she says. "We're—we're a family again. I feel it. You feel it, don't you?"

I feel a possibility. I feel her longing for what she had, and how she now sees possibilities beyond that. Sees me.

I nod, and then ask a question I have to ask. "Does— what happened to Sophy?"

"Sophy?" Jane says. "What do you mean?"

"I mean, how come she's—" I break off, because Jane doesn't know what I'm talking about.

But I know what to do. I was trained to find things out.

"I just—I heard she's been in trouble," I said. "That she's—I don't know. Someone said she tried to hurt someone or something like that."

"Sophy?" Jane says, and shakes her head. "No, that's not possible. She's so quiet. She's—she's just waiting. She'll bloom when she goes to college, but now she just wants to be Greer."

I nod, but I know Sophy wants more than that. Her heart is still the same. It's just—it can't run free in this world, which is a very good thing.

But it doesn't mean I won't be careful.

Sophy comes to pick me up, smiling fake bright, and I kiss Jane's cheek again before I leave. "See you later."

"So, you're getting along with your mom now?" Sophy says as we walk to her car. She greeted Jane with a wide, soft smile that Jane saw nothing but kindness in. I wonder if that's how my mother, my Jane, was. If that's why she wasn't able to see what her choices cost her until it was too late.

"It doesn't take much to make her happy," I say, and watch Sophy's smile. See it for what it is, gleaming and dreaming of prey. Of power.

I wonder how she failed to get it now.

"I should loose my memory, then," Sophy says. "Maybe then someone would notice me."

"I see who you are," I say, and Sophy stares at me.

I stare back and wait, calm and knowing. I understand what this is. I know what people who want power are like and I know her.

I know what to do, know how to stay safe around her.

Sophy looks away first. "Should we go?"

We do, and as we drive to the party I wonder what makes Sophy want to be someone everyone knows and fears so badly. I wonder what made her want it before. I wonder what makes her want it now.

At the party, I see Sophy measure Olivia's desperate, unseen love. I watch her watch Greer posture, posing for one boy and another, always turning to Olivia and stopping her whenever Olivia gets upset enough to finally start to walk away.

I watch, and I finally realize what Sophy—the one I knew, and the one I see now—really wanted. It was more than power. I see that as she stares at Greer and Olivia, and the sparks the two of them don't see but I do. That Sophy does.

Sophy wanted power, but she also wanted love. Not from Olivia or Greer, but from everyone. She wanted—wants—to be noticed. To be the person everyone fears and yet still, deep in their hearts, wants to see.

She wants everything. Power. Love—no, worship.

"Let's go get a drink," she says, turning to me, and then tugs me into another room, pushing a cup into my hand.

"I saw you looking at Greer," she says. "I know you

see how she is, how she tells us what to do, what to wear, how to act, how to think. Even if you don't remember before, you see it now. And if we can just get her to do something stupid, I—we—can be—"

"No," I say, and my voice comes out harsher than I mean it to, but I can't help it. This Sophy did not destroy my world, but the one I know, the one who saw what people wanted to keep hidden and knew what to do in a way this one never will—she did.

She told Clementine about me.

She's why I'm here.

"No?" she says, and in that instant she looks like the Sophy I remember. Sounds like the Sophy I know.

"No," I say again, and she swallows, looks into the other room, looks at Greer standing smiling at people, Olivia flitting around her.

"I knew you'd do this," she hisses. "And you know what? That's fine. I'm sick of pretending I like any of you. Get Greer to take you home tonight, if she's willing. And don't even think of coming to me when she isn't."

I say nothing, and she turns away, then whirls back to face me.

"This is really it?" she says. "We've known each

other for ages, we've put up with being little puppets for ages, and this is fine with you now? This is how you want things to be?"

"I won't hurt anyone for you," I say, not hiding what I know. Who I was. Who I am. I let it shine from my eyes. "Not ever."

She blinks, looking startled, like she's seen something she almost understands but doesn't want to, and then says, "Whatever. Giving you that drink is the last thing I'm ever doing for you."

She turns away again, and this time she doesn't look back, disappears into the shadowy crowd around us. I look and see nothing but tall, dark shapes standing in a row, waiting.

I can guess what happened to the other Ava now. Sophy scared her, she ran, and then the Ava from here died, somehow. Badly, maybe. Easily—I hope so.

But I doubt it.

I see woods, sparse but there, and I see them. I am waiting for Morgan, waiting to leave with him, but he isn't there, just these dark shapes, and someone behind them, someone coming into sight. Someone older, a woman I've never seen before. Clementine.

I see her and—

Blink, and the shadows are just boys, ones I've seen around school, all pimples and eagerness.

But when I was, who I was—then they might have been something else. Might have been people that Sophy arranged to be there. Sent with Clementine as a gift to find me. To make sure I ended up here.

I look at my drink. It's cloudy, smells of liquor and juice and maybe something else. I watch Sophy weave through the boys, nodding at them like the Sophy I knew nodded, all business, all desire to achieve no matter what happened.

I don't know what the Ava I never have been did. But I do know I am not her. I survive, no matter what. It's who I am.

I put my drink down, then bat it away when someone else reaches for it, watch it spill on the floor. Watch Sophy's face twist in fury and then fall.

She is so breakable here and I am glad of it.

I grab Greer's and Olivia's cups, ignoring their pouted protests, and get them new ones.

"I hadn't even had a sip of that," Greer says. "Olivia hadn't touched hers either. I made Sophy get them, and you—look, I thought you didn't remember things. You didn't say you were going to act like a retard in public too."

"Hey, I thought getting drinks was a nice thing to do," Ethan says, coming up behind Greer and smiling at me.

"Ethan," Greer says, throwing her arms around him and snuggling up against him, turning so I can see her triumphant-looking eyes. Next to her, Olivia blows out a breath and then downs her drink in one swift swallow, throat working, eyes closed.

"Good to see you too, Greer," Ethan says, pushing away from her, his body tense. "Hi, Ava."

"Sorry I'm a retard," I say to Greer, who frowns, not sure from my voice if I mean the words or not.

"I was kidding, Ava, duh," Greer says, and looks at Olivia, who is holding her now-empty cup upside down. "Oh shit. Olivia, did you just drink all that? You had one already when we came in, remember?"

"Ava isn't a retard," Olivia says, her voice slurred. "But sometimes you are." She covers her mouth with one hand, as if she's shocked, and then starts to giggle.

"How much liquor did you put in there?" Greer asks me. "You know Olivia is a fucking lightweight."

"I guess she is," I say, and Greer scowls and walks off with Olivia, one arm around her to hold her up, palm resting against Olivia's skin where her shirt has ridden up.

Ethan watches them go and then turns to me, taking a sip of Greer's untouched drink.

"That lemon-lime soda," he says after a moment, grinning. "It's a killer. Poor Olivia."

"I think she'll be all right," I say, and he puts the soda down, touches my arm and turns me gently toward him.

"Me too," he says. "I saw Sophy stomping off just now, and since I saw you come in with her I wanted to make sure you were okay. Not that I was watching you—all right, I was watching you." He grins again, running a hand through his hair, and I watch it fall back into place, hanging so it almost covers his eyes, making him look like a secret waiting to be told.

"For me?" I say, wishing the Ethan I remember, pale and nervous, could have been like this. Could have talked so easily. Could have had a life that was good. Free.

"You want to get out of here?" he says, and I see Sophy glaring at me from the corner, a tiny spider whose web won't set.

Who won't trap me now.

I nod and he smiles, then takes my hand and leads me outside.

"Ava!" I hear as I am opening his car door, and look behind me, see Sophy coming toward us.

"Hey," she says, panting slightly as she reaches me. "Where are you going?"

"Away," I say, and can't control my smile as I get in the car. As I shut the door, sealing myself inside. Sealing myself away from her.

"She looks pissed," Ethan says as we drive off.

I look back. She's still standing there, watching us, a frown wrinkling her face. I wave at her, and she turns away. I see her look down, shake her head, and then rub her eyes.

I guess now I know where all the tears I never saw Sophy shed are, and almost feel sorry for her.

Almost.

"Do you drink coffee?" Ethan says, and I don't see why the other Ava's heart beat faster for him, I will never see it, but I do see someone I know. Someone I remember.

"Sure," I say, and smile at him.

He smiles back, sweetly, the exact smile of the

Ethan I know—the smile I almost never saw—and we drive into the night. Leaving Greer and Olivia and their drama behind. Leaving Sophy and her plans that I won't have to ever know—other than that here, they were nothing compared to what I know—behind.

46.

WE DRIVE TO A COFFEE PLACE, bright and filled with people.

"I think it's more crowded then Brent's party," Ethan says as we pull into the parking lot, and when I look at him, he looks a little overwhelmed. The Ethan I knew looked that way all the time.

We are waiting in line to find out what our assignments will be. Ethan is standing behind me, looking nervous. Overwhelmed.

"You're going to be fine," I say. "You're someone, and if you want, I can go wait at the back of the line. I mean, we've always talked, but now I'm—I'm still going to be the girl from the crèche, you know. The one who was taken in to show that people like me can actually be taught."

"You're my friend," Ethan says. "And you're a survivor. Maybe I want that to rub off on me. I know you know about my test scores."

I make a face at him, and he smiles, then whispers that Greer and Olivia are coming over, their assignments al-

ready in hand. "Brace yourself," he says. "Aren't they so happy you can't stand it?"

"Jealous," I say, and he shakes his head. "I don't—I already know love doesn't exist. I just . . . I want them to be okay. You—will you help me with that?"

I look at him and then nod once, fast.

"Ava," he says, and—

"Ava?" Ethan says now, touching my arm, and I can almost hear the silence in the hall where we stood, can almost see the joy on Greer's and Olivia's faces. I can still feel the want that was in me then, the way I was so sure that getting an assignment would let me know what my life would be.

But then I found out. I found out what I was, who I was going to be . . . and then I met Morgan.

I met Morgan, and everything changed. Love does exist.

And now all I have are memories of it.

"Sorry," I say. "I was just . . . I was just thinking that you're right, it is crowded in there."

"I could make you coffee," he says. "At my house, I mean. If you want. Not that I—I mean, we'd be in my house, but I'd never try—"

"I know," I say, touching his arm, because I do. This Ethan, the one the other Ava loved, is not so different from the one I knew. I wonder why she didn't see how anxious he was under all his beauty.

Maybe she did, and that's why she liked him. I wish . . .

I wish I could feel like she did, I wish I could just slide into her life, but I can't, I won't.

I don't want to.

I remember Morgan still, and too well. I remember love. I still feel it, the way it made me believe anything was possible. The way it set me free, opened up a world I hadn't known I could ever have.

"You know, you're not—you were different before you lost your memory," Ethan says. "More . . . I don't know."

"More innocent," I say without thinking, still half locked in the world I know. In my memories of Morgan.

"No, not that. You were—you were happier," he says, and touches my arm quickly, gently. "Forget coffee, okay? I'll make us some hot chocolate, if you want. I like hot chocolate more than coffee anyway." He grins at me. "Of course, if you tell anyone at school I said that, I'll deny it."

The Ethan I know never had the luxury of making a joke of any kind. He was cowed; anxious and then trapped by whoever it was that saw him, wanted him, and took him. At least here, in this place, someone is happy, and maybe he can teach me how. Maybe I can watch him and learn. Maybe—I can't leave Morgan behind, I will never forget him, but maybe I can find a place here. Maybe I can find a way that will let me live in this world in peace.

"I promise, your secret is safe with me," I say, and we leave the bright, bustling coffeehouse and head back into the night.

47.

ETHAN'S HOUSE IS BEAUTIFUL, hidden up a steep driveway cut into a hill, a long, low wooden building nestled high up among a carefully cultivated body of trees.

"It's gorgeous," I breathe, and it is; it's like the forest is just around the house but in it and it makes me think of waiting for Morgan, of waiting to leave the city, to start our lives together.

I wonder if everything will always somehow remind me of him.

"You think?" Ethan says, turning the car off before we even get close to the garage. "I don't get the whole log cabin in the sky thing, actually. But then, I'm not a million years old like my stepfather."

He turns the car off and looks at the dark house for a moment.

"I'm pretty sure everyone's asleep," he finally says. "You don't mind being quiet, do you? I don't want— I hate the questions that come when people wake up and find out someone's come over or something, you know?"

I nod because I understand. I know questions.

Who are you? What are you doing here?

I heard those question asked before, in another place, a place where I was truly me. I never asked them—I was never trusted like that—but I heard how people sounded when their dreams were shattered, when their lives were turned into a waking nightmare.

And beyond that, back to that very first night, to opening my eyes and seeing the nothing that lay beyond them. Feeling the nothing. *Who am I? Where am I?*

Wake up, I thought then, *wake up,* but I couldn't, I was already awake.

I was here.

Ethan's house is dark, but I can see that it's huge and open, all tall ceilings and long walls that seem to stretch out into the trees themselves, walls made of glass that take the night sky, the dark trees, and absorb their darkness, casting it as darker shadows all around us.

"Careful," he whispers, touching my arm as we tiptoe down the hall, and this is what being other Ava is like, this what she would have wanted, the simple, silly joy of creeping down a hall in a beautiful house with a boy.

The kitchen is all gleaming steel, shining even in the faint light that Ethan switches on, casting a soft puddle of light around the stove and leaving the glass wall and windows, all the rest, dark.

He makes the hot chocolate with ease, putting generous spoonfuls of it into milk and then heating it on the stove. There is a microwave behind him, gleaming like the rest of the kitchen, and when he sees me looking at it he smiles and says, "The stove is quieter. And besides, things should—they should be real sometimes, you know?"

He hands me a cup full of dark, delicious-smelling liquid. He pours another one for himself, turning the stove off and coming to stand next to me.

"Better than coffee," he says after he takes a sip and I take one too. It is better than coffee, sweeter and richer, and creamy, and I start to tell him that, start to say thank you, when Ethan hunches into himself, turning into the Ethan I know right in front of me as he stares past me.

Stares down the hallways that lead out of the kitchen. That led us in here.

"I didn't—I thought you'd be asleep," he says, and his voice is quiet. Scared.

"Who is this?" a voice, back in the dark hallway, back in the shadow of glass and wood, says, and I feel my skin prickle, a weird skittering sensation crawling through me.

"Just a friend," Ethan says, and puts his cup down. His hand is shaking as he does. "Is Mom awake?"

"No, she's asleep. She had a long day." A man steps into the kitchen, tall and wide, with shoulders that look like they could hold up the sky. He slides one glance at me—dismissive but angry—and then looks back at Ethan. "You know you aren't supposed to bring guests here without permission."

"Mom doesn't care if people come over," Ethan says, and he is standing straight and tall again but all around him, everywhere I look, I see the Ethan I know, shrunken and scared, trapped in a place he didn't want to be, gifted with everything he could ever want but expected to give so much—everything—in return.

"I care," the man says, walking into the room, filling it, short gray hair, striped pajamas, a dad like I've seen on television with Jane, over-worried and carefully checking to make sure Ethan is okay.

Too carefully.

He's looking at him like he owns him. Like everything Ethan is, inside and out, belongs to him.

"I—I need to take Ava home," Ethan says, taking a step back toward me, not to shield me, but as if I am shielding him, as if standing near me means something. Shows something. "I'll be back in a little while, I promise."

"Ava?" the man says and comes into the room fully, comes into the light, and I don't know him. I have never seen him—not even in my memories—but I don't want to be near him. His eyes, his walk, everything about him, screams that this is someone who knows how to succeed. Who gets everything he wants. "You never said anything to me about an Ava. About anyone. You know I don't like that. You know I don't like lies."

Who is dangerous.

"I do need to get back to—back to Jane," I say. "She's my—she's waiting up for me. I'm sorry if I—"

"You don't have anything to be sorry for," the man says gently, as if he is just a dad, and I'm so wound up from Sophy and things I remember, things that aren't here, that I must be seeing things, must be—

The man hits Ethan. Casually, carelessly, as if it's nothing. As if he's done it so many times before that it requires no thought. As if Ethan's nothing.

I think of Ethan's photos, then. All those open, lonely spaces. All those places where no one else was around.

He is trapped too.

Ethan is forever, always trapped. Even in this shiny world, he's lost too.

"You know how I feel about you bringing people here," the man says. "You know this house is mine. You know everything in it is mine." He leans in toward Ethan and Ethan doesn't move away, doesn't run, doesn't flinch, just stands still, frozen. "Now say it."

"It's yours, it's all yours," Ethan says, his voice gone distant, numb, and I know that voice, I know the face he's making, the one that sees but doesn't, the one that exists but doesn't really live. "I'm yours. Just—just let me take her home and I'll come back right away, I promise. I swear."

"Good," the man says, and smiles at me, actually

smiles at me, like I don't know what he is, like I don't see the rot inside him. "Have a good night, Ava."

"Come on," Ethan says, his voice low, barely a mutter, barely anything, broken, and this can't be what I have to live in, this can't be the world I have to be in, everything is still so wrong, still so full of anger and fear.

I don't want this.

"Hurry back, Ethan," the man says, smiling, his teeth all white and ready to snap. Ethan takes my arm and I stop.

"No," I say, "you don't get to—you're nothing. Nothing."

Ethan looks back at me, his eyes huge and scared and sorry and I know that look, I have seen it—but where? when?—and then, when the man stares at me, violence in his eyes, Ethan is shoving him, hitting him, fists flying, pounding, and the man is staggering back, shocked and reeling into the wall, glass cracking under him, around him.

"You little weasel," he says. "You little nothing."

And then he shoves Ethan, shoves him hard, cocks a fist and smashes it into Ethan's face. Ethan rocks back, stumbling into me, dropping to his knees as I am falling away, back into the dark, into the wall of glass behind me, a strange splintering noise in my ears, pain all around, all over, and I have been here before, I have seen Ethan turning toward me with that look on his face, so scared and so sorry and then the memory is there, all around me, *Ethan looking at me, shaking his head, and I see sorrow in his eyes, real sorrow, and then Clementine waves one hand and he is pulled away, grasped tight by large, hairy hands, hands sticking out of a government uniform, hands that pull Ethan away, drag him into the woods, and I hear Ethan sobbing but I want Morgan, I only want Morgan but he isn't here and—*

And then I am falling, down through glass and into the night sky.

Ethan was the one who led Clementine to me. Who helped her send me here. Not Sophy, for all her scheming, for all her plans. Ethan, with his shadowed, desperate eyes, so eager to be free.

Ethan did this.

Did this then.

And now—

I saw how the house was built when we came, glass nestled high up in the trees, the ground so far below, and Jane didn't know what happened to her Ava, Clementine didn't give her that moment, that memory, and she thought I was safe now, I thought I was safe now, I thought I understood this world but I didn't, I don't and—

Clementine knelt over me once. Pressed her hand to my forehead. My eyes fluttered closed as pain tore through me.

Again and again it came and is happening once more, happening now, pain and then dark and then nothing.

48.

WAKE UP.

"Ava," I hear, "Ava" and Morgan is there, arms wrapped around me, holding me tight and it was a dream, it was all a dream, I didn't leave, I wasn't sent away, we are together, we are safe, and I reach for his face but can't touch it, my fingers slide through it and he smiles at me, lips brushing against my ear but I don't feel it, I don't feel the warmth of his skin I just feel air, cold air, and I tell myself to wake up, *wake up.*

I see light up above us, faint light shining through glass, two figures staring down at us and it happened, it's real, I'm here, I fell, I hurt, I do, and Morgan—

"Morgan?" I say, and it comes out all strange, bur-bled and broken.

"I couldn't go," Morgan says. "I had to—I couldn't leave you, Ava. You would never leave me."

"But you—you're—" I reach for him again and my hand slips across him as if there is nothing to him, as if he is water, as if he is mist, unreal. Fading into dust.

"I love you," he says, as if it explains everything, as

if it is everything, and then his eyes go strange, look at me but don't see me. Look as if . . . look as if they see nothing.

"Morgan," I say again, pleading, and my hands slide though him and his eyes are open, they are still open but they aren't moving, they aren't blinking, they are looking at me but they aren't seeing me. He is still here but I can't feel him, there is nothing to him, and all around me the world pushes darker and darker, fading, and he was supposed to go, I told him to go, and he can't—

"Morgan," I scream, my voice hurting, all of me hurting, and he stares at me but doesn't see me.

Doesn't see anything.

I scream again and again and then the world pushes me down, pushes me into the dark. Pushing and pushing and I can't reach Morgan, I can't even see him, I can't—

49.

WAKE UP.

I hear a beeping noise, loud and steady and mechanical. Fake. I listen to it, so sure in its simple metallic beat, and then Morgan comes back, comes into my mind, and I open my eyes. Look for him.

Jane is leaning over me, and when I see her, she smiles, mouth wide and cracking full of joy.

"Ava," she says, "oh, Ava, honey, I knew you'd wake up, I just knew it," and puts her arms around me, pain in my side in my arms in my back all around me. All I am.

"Where's Morgan?" I say.

Jane looks at me, right at me, for a moment, and then looks away.

I grab her hand. It is warm in mine, the skin soft.

"Jane," I say, and I never got to touch my mother's hand like this, not ever, she was taken away before I could understand who she was, before I could see that she loved me. Before I knew what love was. "What happened to Morgan?"

"You mean the boy who—the one who was there when you fell," she says. "The one who I saw following you."

She knows what happened, she knows who he is to me, I can see it in her eyes. She knows everything, she sees that I came to her with a head filled with a life she wasn't in. She sees that I remember him, that he was in my memories. That my heart beat for him and still does.

And she knows where he is now. I see it. I know it.

"Tell me," I whisper, and she leans over, resting her head on my shoulder as if she needs me to hold her.

"You fell out of a window—out of a house—and when you did, that boy, Morgan, was—he was—"

I remember how there was almost nothing to him. I remember the light in his eyes, I remember how it dimmed, how he looked at me but didn't.

He said he loved me. That he knew I would never leave him.

"Tell me," I say, and my voice is rising, the beeping around me rising too, growing shriller, sharper.

"There was a—when you fell, Morgan was standing right where you landed. You—you broke your legs and an arm and a few bones in your back, and there's internal bleeding, but you'll be all right, you're here, and I swear I won't ever—"

I grab her arm, squeeze. "What happened to Morgan?"

She closes her eyes.

"He died," she says, her voice quiet. "When you fell, he was somehow—he was exactly where you landed. He—you would have died if he wasn't there. He broke your fall, but there was . . . there was a rock and they say his head hit it and—"

She is still talking but I can't hear her. I can't hear her because I see the light in his eyes again, I see it dimming again and he didn't leave when I told him to.

Morgan stayed, he stayed for me.

He died for me, he said I would never leave him, that he knew me, and he came to get me and stayed and I am alive, I am breathing because of him.

I want to scream but I can't because I'm hurting. All of me, body and soul, is hurting.

I can't scream because my pain is too big to be let out.

If I scream it would travel through this room, this place, through everything. It would travel through the universe itself, through every me in every place and I was so sure I understood things, I was so sure Morgan was safe, that I was safe, but I was wrong.

I was wrong then, I am wrong now.

I hear the beeping noise again, and turn my head slowly, painfully, see it is all the equipment around me talking slowly, steadily. One, two, three, beep.

Like a heart, and I wish mine wasn't beating. I told Morgan to go but he didn't, he stayed, and now—

No. I don't want to think that his eyes are closed forever everywhere.

I have survived the crèche, the SAT, Clementine, all of it, and for . . .

For Morgan to die.

Morgan.

My eyes burn. My body screams.

"Don't close your eyes," my mother whispers and it is my mother, Jane is my mother, here and there and in my heart forever and everywhere I can ever be. "I know you're in pain, but the doctors are coming. They said you might not wake up but I knew you would, Ava. I knew you'd come back to me. I swore to Clementine that if you did I would never ever let you go."

"You have to," I say, and grab her hand, hard. "You have to let me—I want to go."

I do. I don't want—I just want to go. I don't want to be—

Morgan.

"We'll go home soon," she says, blinking hard, her eyes not meeting mine. "I swear you'll be okay, you're going to make it," and the beeping grows louder, faster, and I squeeze tighter, harder, pleading without words.

Her eyes go wide, and she shakes her head.

"Ava," she says. "You're here, you're still here, I know it hurts but the doctors really are coming and—"

"Let me go," I tell her, the words coming out thick, slow. Pleading. "If you love me, let me go. Let *her* go. If you do, I can be free. I don't—you know I shouldn't be here."

"Ava," she says, finally looking at me, and her tears fall on my face. They don't taste like salt or rain. They don't taste like anything.

"Please," I whisper. "Mommy, please."

She closes her eyes then, bends down so her forehead touches mine.

"I love you," she says. "You don't know how much I love you."

50.

WAKE UP.

Dark, so dark, all I see are stars above me glittering bright. I know them.

Suck in a breath, my lungs starved for air, and Morgan is looking down at me, trees all around him. All around us, their dark branches shadowing the night.

"Ava," he says, and it sounds like a song, his voice full of joy, full of life, and he touches my cheek, my mouth, presses his lips to my forehead. "Are you all right?"

"Morgan?" I say, wanting to believe I see him, that he's here, but I'm afraid to.

"I came early," he says. "I don't know why I did, but I felt this . . . thing. Like I had to get here, you know? And when I did, you were—you were on the ground and . . . I don't know. You looked like you were asleep, but you wouldn't wake up. I thought about—there's someone I know, that I could ask for help, maybe, but I—I didn't want to leave you. I just . . . I knew you'd wake up. That you'd come back to me."

I reach up and touch his hand, feel the warmth of

his fingers against my face. "You're here," I breathe. "You're—you're really here."

"Where else would I be?" he says, and smiles at me. "I'm glad we're away from the city. Glad we're here, and safe, but I—the someone I know, I have to tell you about them. I have to tell you about my family."

"It's all right," I say, and twine my fingers through his. "I know."

"You know?"

I nod.

"I—Ava," Morgan says. "I should have told you before, but I—I was afraid that if you knew Clementine was my grandmother that you'd think I was like her. I . . . you really know? And you still want to be here? With me?"

"Yes," I say. "I know you, know your heart. I'll always know you. I love you."

He kisses me then, gently, and whispers, "I was so scared when I got here and saw you, but now . . ." He grins at me, and I see how much he loves me in that smile, I see everything so clearly. I see forever. "Now you have to promise you're not going anywhere without me, okay?"

"Never," I say, and close my eyes.

Acknowledgments

Many thanks for everyone at Dutton, especially Julie Strauss-Gabel and Rosanne Lauer.

Jess, thanks for reading so many drafts, and huge hugs to Clara and Amy for their time and thoughts as well. And Diana, I'd have been lost without your pointing out that one word I was missing!

As always, thanks to Robin Rue and Beth Miller for all they do.

Finally, thank *you* for reading Ava's story!

**Continue reading for a glimpse of
Elizabeth Scott's gripping novel**

I'm afraid my hair is showing. Chris said the dye would work but I'm not sure he much cared if it did; and I don't think it was true dye, just a mixture of color he'd created, a kind of a paint and nothing more. Plus the train is hot, so hot the floor burns my feet, little red huff hisses of pain searing up into my legs.

I want to get off this train but I can't. Not now. It is the only choice left to me, and it is actually considered an honor to be here. To be trusted enough to be on this train, to have a ticket for it, is something most can't even dare to dream of. Keran Berj lets few people out of this land—his land, or so he says—and only those on government business are allowed to go. And then only if the business will result in glory of some kind for Keran Berj.

I'm certainly not supposed to have the honor of being on this train.

I'm not supposed to be here at all.

Chris made my hair glow over a sink, frowning when I tried to move away from the scissors in his hand. The gold I'd given him to help me had bought me no trust and only a tiny bit of his patience.

So now I worry that the bright color is bleeding, raining off my hair and onto my skin. Stupidly, I worry that it is staining my shirt. It is white, with buttons made of tin. One of the sleeves has been sewn in crooked, a large gathered fold lying where my shoulder is.

I've never had a shirt made by machines before.

Inside the fold is space for three of my fingers, like a hiding place in the open, an error made by the machine that sewed the shirt. I was fascinated by it for a while, slipped my fingers into it when we first got on the train until Kerr, the boy Chris made me wait for, the one who I must pretend is my brother, kicked me in the ankle, hard, and hissed, "Stop acting like a piece of Hill shit," as he pretended to be checking the lumpy, stained seat waiting for us.

It's an insult here, in this world. In Keran Berj's world. To be from the Hills is an insult. I hate that, even as I know I would never go back there.

Can't go back there.

Once this train was very grand, or so the stories go. Before Keran Berj, who supposedly rules us all, there was someone else, someone who truly did command everyone's loyalty, a great man who ruled from far away. He is said to have had the strength of a bear and the wisdom of the Saints. He came only once a year to take money and did not crack the dead's teeth to pull out their fillings and melt them into statues. This man came and rode everywhere—from the mountains to the seas—in a long, beautiful train. Its insides were covered with diamonds, and at night it shone brighter than the stars.

Then the man died. No one else came to rule—we were forgotten—and Keran Berj stepped forward and said he would lead, that everyone would be equals and life would be better.

I wonder if it is a rule that all stories must end with a lie. But then, the only stories I know are the ones the People tell, and they all end with Keran Berj and his false words, so maybe there are some that don't.

It is so hot. My hair is wet when I push my fingers into it, my feet hurt, and the man in front of us smells like onions, the wild ones that grow on the side of the Hills. The ones you can smell before you see them, the ones that start to grow with the promise of spring. I can hardly believe this train was grand once, but I see hints of it in the markings where things have been pried away, decorations and comforts removed for someone else's use.

Keran Berj's use. No one will mention this, though. The train is—and will always be—called glorious in spite of its sad state, because not only do you never know who is watching, you never know who is listening. Even those trusted enough to have tickets for this train, this trip, watch what they do. What they say. The train is special, and so is everyone on it, but no one is above Keran Berj.

No one.

At least, according to him.

"Are you asleep, sister?" Kerr asks, and puts his hand on my elbow, stilling my fingers as they twist through my damp hair.

"No," I say, and lower my hand, place it in my

lap on top of my fake papers. There is no stain on my fingers. The dye holds. When I am safely across the border, the first thing I will do is leave Kerr behind.

I would kill him, but I already know I am too weak for that.